KU-467-208

To my hearty crew of nephews

and nieces xxxx - JM

DUNDEE CITY
COUNCIL

ATION

CENTRAL CHILDREN'S

ESSION NUMBER
CO/082 323X

PLIER   PRICE
ASIC   £5.99

CLASS No.   DATE
               24/11/22

First published in Great Britain 2022
by New Frontier Publishing Europe Ltd
Vine House, 58-60 Kensington Church Street, London W8 4DB
www.newfrontierpublishing.co.uk

ISBN: 978-1-915167-30-9

Text copyright © 2022 Jenny Moore
Illustration copyright © 2022 Elisa Paganelli
Endpapers © Digital Curio
All rights reserved.

The rights of Jenny Moore to be identified as the author and Elisa Paganelli
to be identified as the illustrator of this work have been asserted.

This book is sold subject to the condition that it shall not, by way of trade
or otherwise, be lent, hired out or otherwise circulated in any form of binding or
cover other than that in which it is published. No part of this publication may be
reproduced, stored in a retrieval system, or transmitted, in any form or by any means
(electronic, mechanical, photocopying, recording or otherwise), without the prior
written permission of New Frontier Publishing Europe Ltd.

A CIP catalogue record for this book
is available from the British Library.

Edited by Tasha Evans • Designed by Verity Clark

Printed and bound in Turkey
1 3 5 7 9 10 8 6 4 2

ODELIA
AND THE VARMINT

JENNY MOORE

Illustrations by Elisa Paganelli

NEW FRONTIER PUBLISHING

Our Hearty Cast and Crew

Odelia Hardluck-Smythe
A brave and resourceful young hero who'll do anything to save her family. Keen to swap toast for treasure.

Captain Blunderfuss
A rude and smelly pirate with a secret heart of gold. Loves marzipan fruits and velvet trousers.

Mrs Hardluck-Smythe
Odelia's widowed mother. A hard-working writer, struggling to keep a roof over her family's head.

Cook and Cat the Dog
The sleepiest pirate to sail the seventeen seas and his trusty one-eared cat ... called Dog.

SAMMY HARDLUCK-SMYTHE

Odelia's smiley baby brother.
The one ray of light in
her lonely life since her
father's tragic death.

ADMIRAL ARBUCKLE
(AKA MR BUGWELL)

Captain Blunderfuss's
smart-trousered nemesis.
A so-called expert on
woodworm infestations.

MRS PONSONBY-SMARM

The Hardluck-Smythes'
haughty next-door neighbour.
Keeper of ornamental carp.

SERGEANT THATAWAY

A local policeman on the hunt
for the notorious Mayfair Mob.
A keen birdwatcher.

CHAPTER 1

Mayfair, London, 1890

The *number one* worst part of not having a father any more, thought eleven-year-old Odelia Harmony Hardluck-Smythe, was everything. She missed the big boom of his voice and the stiff tickle of his waxed moustache. She missed his pig-like snorts of disbelief as he perused the morning papers – *Good heavens, whatever is the world coming to?* – and the stray sprinklings of smoked kipper on his waistcoat. She missed his tuneless humming, the fog-like steam of his spectacles when he came huffing in from the cold and the sweet, comforting smell of his snuff box.

She even missed his scoldings – *Come now, Odelia. That's no way to talk about our neighbour, is it? She can't help being a poisonous old bag with a face like a rhinoceros's backside.* And she really, really, *really* missed the special goodnights he whispered into her hair as she snuggled down under her silken bedcovers. *Sleep well, little Oddy Odd Sock*, he'd say, ruffling snuff-scented fingers through her freshly brushed hair. It was a long time since Odelia had been *anyone's* odd sock. It was a long time since anyone had brushed her hair, come to that. Even the silken bedcovers were a distant memory now, sold to the tailor on Rotherford Street to help pay for the funeral.

Yes, Odelia concluded, pushing her dark, knotty curls out of her face and spearing another slice of bread with her toasting fork, the first worst thing about not having a father any more *was everything*. And the *second* worst thing about Mr Hardluck-Smythe's sudden departure from life was not having a mother any more either. At least, not in any real, mothering sense of the word. Mrs Hardluck-Smythe was so busy working on her new children's book, in a desperate effort to keep a roof over their heads, that Odelia barely saw her at all. Entire weeks might drift past with nothing more in the way of conversation than a murmured 'Morning, Oddy' over a breakfast of stale toast, and a weary 'Evening, Oddy' over a supper of even staler toast.

Mrs Hardluck-Smythe had been slaving over her pirate book for months now, holed up in the nursery at the mahogany writing desk she'd inherited from her husband. And as much as Odelia missed spending time with her, she couldn't help admiring her mother's determination – a determination to write her way out of their spiralling debts. But Mr Pickfill the publisher had already turned down her first book … what if he didn't like this one either?

The tall Mayfair townhouse, with its large sash windows and colourful William Morris-patterned wallpaper, used to be a warm, happy place. But now, with Mr Hardluck-Smythe and all the servants gone – not to mention half the furniture – it felt cold and empty. Dreamy summer afternoons spent listening to the new gramophone or playing croquet on the lawn belonged to a different world now. So did cosy evenings cuddled up by the fire, eating hot buttered crumpets and listening to Mr Hardluck-Smythe reading *Treasure Island*. Mayfair itself, with its grand mansions and elegant mews, seemed to belong to a different world too, now that life had taken such a dark, lonely turn. Or rather *Odelia* belonged to a different world – a poor, fatherless world at odds with the fancy streets and wealthy inhabitants beyond her own four walls. A world that was growing poorer with every passing day.

She sat at the breakfast table as she did each morning, missing her father and their old way of life, and watching the stale toast turn soggy. She'd been sitting like that – staring at the half-burnt bread until the toasting fork patterns swam into tiny jeering faces – for the last twenty minutes, reluctant to start eating until her mother arrived. In truth, her reluctance had more to do with the spread before her than an unwanted attack of good manners. There was only so much stale toast a poor fatherless child could stomach in one lifetime. Unfortunately, toast was the only thing Odelia knew how to cook – indeed the *only* thing the Hardluck-Smythes had left to cook – so it was pretty much toast or nothing. And if the kindly baker who gave away his day-old leftover loaves each morning had no leftover loaves to give away, then nothing was exactly what the Hardluck-Smythes got.

Finally, when the backless grandfather clock started its extra-loud eight o'clock chimes (the back having been sacrificed for firewood, one finger-nipping frosty morning a few months before), Odelia decided enough was enough.

'Enough's enough,' she announced to the indifferent pile of toast beside her, dropping her hands to her hips for added emphasis.

The toast said nothing.

'If Mother's too busy to come to me, I shall have to go to her instead,' she told the teapot.

'Why, that's an excellent idea,' said the teapot encouragingly. 'A tea and toast picnic in the nursery might be exactly what she needs.' At least, that's what Odelia would have said, if she were a teapot. In reality, the teapot stayed as silent and superior as ever, the turned-up curve of his spout suggesting he was above such tedious breakfast time discussions.

'Good,' said Odelia. 'That's settled then. It's a shame we burned the tea tray… I'll have to improvise.'

She headed to the scullery at the back of the house where Hetty, their faithful family maid, used to clean the family's clothes and dishes, and looked around for inspiration. Hetty was long gone now and the huge hot and cold sinks stood empty. There were no clothes soaking in the dolly tub and no water being wrung out at the once-busy mangle. Odelia picked up a washboard, meaning to try it out for size, but her latest attempt at doing the family laundry had left it far too slippery with soap for any breakfast-carrying. She settled instead on an old tin roasting pan, piling it high with cold tea and toast and placing a pretty weed, that had worked its way through the floorboards, into a milk jug in place of actual milk. And then she carried it, wobbling all over the place, through the house and up the stairs, oblivious to the trail of brown drips following along behind her.

The damp nursery had doubled up as the study ever since they'd let Nanny go, allowing Odelia's mother to mind the baby and write at the same time. Not that Samuel Rochester Hardluck-Smythe *needed* much minding. He was a cheerful, placid creature who liked nothing better than lying in his crib and playing with his own feet. He cried when he was hungry, of course, or wet, or soiled, but for the rest of the time he was all smiles and gurgles, beaming at the mould patches on the ceiling as if they were priceless works of art. He smiled at the silverfish scuttling up the nursery wall. Smiled at the scratchy blanket that chafed his chilly limbs. Smiled at the dark circles under his mother's eyes and the smell of burnt toast seeping through the house like a charred vengeance. Not even his father's absence could dent his cheerful demeanour. Having first put in an appearance a mere day after Mr Hardluck-Smythe toppled into the Thames, little Sammy didn't miss him at all. And why would he? He'd never known the tickle of his father's moustache or the smell of his snuff box, completely content to pass his days without smoked kipper sprinklings or scoldings or even a single sock-based term of endearment.

Sammy gurgled a greeting as Odelia bumped and battled her way into the cluttered room with her laden roasting tin, stubbing her toe on the carved wooden rocking horse with the falling-out mane and sending the zoetrope flying off the bookcase onto the floor. It was a cheery kind of Sammy greeting, somewhere between a hiccup and a burp, with a burst of broken wind thrown in for good measure, but Odelia was too busy staring at the nursery window to answer. Too busy staring at the tall, shadowy shape lurking behind the moth-eaten red curtains …

What on earth …? She blinked in confusion. *No! It can't be … can it?*

'Morning, Oddy,' Mrs Hardluck-Smythe glanced up from her ink-splodged scribblings, peering through her *pince nez* at Odelia. 'Gosh, is it breakfast time already?' she asked with unusual chattiness, oblivious to the man-shaped figure behind her scarlet drapes.

But Odelia couldn't tear her eyes away. 'F … F …' she stuttered, her whole body trembling with disbelief. Disbelief and desperate, desperate hope. The roasting tin crashed to the floor, sending tea and toast and broken bits of china careering across the dripped-on rug.

'Oh Oddy,' said Mrs Hardluck-Smythe, shaking her head. 'What shall we do for a teapot now?'

'Hic-urp, hic-urp,' gurgled Sammy, clutching at his toes and grinning.

But Odelia scarcely heard them. 'F … Father!' she cried, stepping over the broken china and running to the window. 'Father, is that you?'

CHAPTER 2

Odelia gasped as the heavy red curtains were wrenched aside, sending clouds of moths fluttering up to the ceiling. It was a long, dramatic gasp – perhaps the longest gasp of her life – running through a whole host of emotions in rapid succession. It began with breathless notes of hope and longing, circling through shock and surprise before plunging down, down, down into the darkest depths of disappointment and fear. It wasn't Mr Hardluck-Smythe come back from the dead to ruffle snuff-scented fingers through her knotted hair. In fact, the hand lunging towards her now as she stood there, mid-gasp, wasn't even a hand. It was a hook.

'You're NOT F-father,' stammered Odelia, catching her hip on the corner of her mother's writing desk as she staggered backwards, away from the hook's glistening spiked tip. 'You're … you're a pirate!'

He certainly *looked* like a pirate, with a salt-encrusted patch over his right eye and a yellowing skull and crossbones adorning his black tricorn hat. The knobbly bits at the end of the bones had started to wear away, but there was no mistaking the grinning skull in the middle, or the 'This Hat Belongs to Captain Blunderfuss' label sticking out of the bottom. He had a bushy brown beard, peppered with ship's biscuit crumbs and slithers of fish tail, and a wooden peg leg peeking out of his raggedy knickerbockers. The only thing missing, in fact, was a parrot on his shoulder squawking 'Pieces of Eight', like Long John Silver's parrot in *Treasure Island*.

'*Father?*' repeated the pirate, his scarred top lip

curling up in distaste. 'Horned pout and halibut! Of course I'm not your father. I'm Captain Blunderfuss, the scourge of the seventeen seas.'

'Dada,' said Sammy unhelpfully, kicking his chubby legs in the air and grinning at the unfolding drama.

Captain Blunderfuss didn't seem to notice. 'Everyone knows who *I* am,' he told Odelia. 'Who the devilfish are *you*? *That's* the real question. And where am I? Who's she?' he added, pointing his hook at Mrs Hardluck-Smythe. 'How did I get here? What happened to my ship? Where did Cook and Dog disappear to? And why is there a smashed teapot on the floor?' It turned out the pirate had *lots* of questions. Once he got going there was no stopping him. 'Is anyone going to eat that toast or not? Have you got any jam? What flavour is it? Don't try giving me raspberry. The pips get stuck in my teeth. Speaking of which …' He reached into the enormous wooden doll's house – a present from Odelia's late grandmother that had escaped being sold or burned on sentimental grounds – and pulled out a beautifully carved dining chair, snapping off one of the legs to use as a toothpick.

'Raspberry pips! How could I forget?' said Mrs Hardluck-Smythe, surprisingly unruffled by the appearance of a raspberry-hating, furniture-snapping pirate from behind the nursery curtains. 'You were still picking them out with your hook when you ran into those rocks off Blind Skull Bay. That's how you ended up with that nasty big hole in your top lip.' She leaned forwards, peering through her *pince nez* at the new arrival. 'Yes,' she murmured. 'I can see the scar from here.'

'How did you know that?' growled Captain Blunderfuss, shielding his lip with his other hand as if the memory was still painful.

'Yes,' echoed Odelia, trying (and failing) to make sense of the situation. 'How *did* you know that?' Her mother was talking as if she'd actually been there when it happened. As if she'd been sailing round Blind Skull Bay (wherever that was) with a piratical pip-picker when disaster struck. But that was impossible.

'Because I wrote it, of course,' said Mrs Hardluck-

Smythe, tapping the ink-splodged manuscript on the desk in front of her. She smiled fondly at the pirate, picking up her fountain pen to resume her work. 'Speaking of which,' she began, 'I really must get this chapter finished before …' She stopped, glancing from the pirate to Odelia and back again. 'Sorry, Oddy, what was that you said? Before, I mean. After the teapot-dropping. It almost sounded like, "You're a pirate."' She shook her head, as if referring to a pirate as a pirate was a preposterous idea.

'That's *exactly* what I said,' Odelia agreed, her poor befuddled brain still struggling to keep up. *What do you mean? How can you have written him?* Captain Blunderfuss wasn't a collection of words on a page, he was a collection of limbs and organs on a rug. A rather odorous collection at that, judging by the waves of sour sweat and sun-baked fish battling with the freshly squeezed aroma emanating from Sammy's undercarriage.

'You can see him too?' Mrs Hardluck-Smythe beamed. Odelia had forgotten how beautiful her mother looked when she smiled. There'd been very little to smile *about* of late and Mrs Hardluck-Smythe had been too busy writing to take much notice of her appearance in general. But even though her high-collared dress was looking worn and shabby now, and her once-coiffed brown curls were falling down in stray strands around her face, Odelia's mother was still a striking woman, especially when she smiled. 'How marvellous,' she said cheerfully. 'And to think that wretched publisher Mr Pickfill called my characters "dull and lifeless" …'

'*You?*' interrupted the pirate, sending a shower of spittle raining down over the mahogany desk. He waved his hook at Odelia's mother. '*You're* the one who wrote me?'

Mrs Hardluck-Smythe nodded, still beaming. 'Mr Pickfill said the witch in my last book was too wishy-washy and wet. He said I needed a better villain if I wanted to get published. And here you are,' she finished. 'Looking every bit as villainous as I'd imagined.'

The pirate didn't seem to share her enthusiasm. 'You mean you're the one who chopped off my hand and gave me an ugly great hook instead? Who swapped a perfectly good leg for an old broom handle? Who squirted poisonous squid ink in my eye, landing me with a patch for the rest of my life?'

'Well … I er …' Mrs Hardluck-Smythe hesitated. She wasn't beaming quite so broadly any more.

'I could have been anyone,' spat Captain Blunderfuss. '*Anyone.* Prime Minister of Great Britain.'

Odelia wasn't so sure about that. She'd seen pictures of the Prime Minister, Lord Salisbury, in the newspaper. He had a big bushy beard, a bit like a pirate, and a tailed coat, but that was as far as the similarities went. He definitely didn't have a battered hat with a skull and crossbones, or bits of old food stuck in his facial hair. As far as she knew, prime ministers didn't jump out from behind the curtains and wave their hooks at people either.

'I could have been a wealthy aristocrat with a handsome country estate and tailored trousers,' Captain Blunderfuss continued. 'Or a toffee-nosed, tailored-trousered naval officer, like my arch-enemy Admiral

Arbuckle, with love-sick ladies swooning at his neatly stitched ankle hems …'

'Dada?' suggested Sammy, not wanting to be left out. In fairness, Mr Hardluck-Smythe *was* rather partial to a fine pair of tailored trousers (at least he had been in his less-deceased days). In fact, it was his resolute belief in the value of such garments – velvet knickerbockers to be precise – that had landed the family in their current economic mess. But Odelia was too busy thinking other, more pressing thoughts at that moment, to reflect on the unfortunate link between gentlemen's leg coverings and the perilous state of her family's finances.

'Dada?' said Sammy again.

Dada? No. Maybe Captain Blunderfuss could have been someone important, if Mother had written him a better role in life. *But he'd still be no match for Father*, thought Odelia as a fresh wave of sadness came barrelling through the initial shock and confusion. To think she'd mistaken the pirate for her beloved parent! The new arrival was everything Mr Hardluck-Smythe wasn't – scruffy, crass and stinky. He was also (rather crucially) still alive. That's to say he wasn't *dead* which was more or less the same thing. Wasn't it? *Oh Father, why did you have to die?*

'I could write you a pair of tailored trousers now if they'd make you feel better,' offered Mrs Hardluck-Smythe, oblivious to her daughter's inner turmoil. 'What colour would you prefer? Black, mauve or peacock blue?'

'Pah!' spat the pirate. 'It'll take more than a pair of trousers to fix *your* sorry mess. My mess I should say, seeing as I'm the one stuck in the middle of it.' He scratched his nose with the tip of his hook. 'No, I'll tell you what you can do, *lady*,' he said, squeezing seven different shades of threat into two otherwise unassuming syllables. 'You can go back to the beginning and write me *properly* this time, with dashing good looks, pots of lovely money and an entire wardrobe of trousers in finest velvet with handstitched piping. Black, mauve *and* peacock blue.' He closed his good eye, lost in his own imaginings.

Mrs Hardluck-Smythe looked singularly unimpressed. 'I'm not sure that–'

The pirate's eye snapped open again. 'Shussh! I haven't finished yet. Make sure you write me like a proper hero this time or there'll be trouble.' He thought for a moment. 'Skip all that bothersome bravery and risking your life for others nonsense though. I mean the kind of hero who stays in bed all day eating marzipan fruits, getting richer and richer without lifting a finger.' He nodded. 'Yes, that's right, *finger* I said. Not *hook*.'

'That doesn't sound very heroic to me,' said Odelia, feeling doubly guilty for having confused such a lazy lout with her fine figure of a father. 'And besides, what would be the point of all those trousers if you never even got out of bed? Surely pyjamas would be more practical?'

'Did I *ask* for your opinion?' snarled the pirate, rounding on her. 'No, I asked for jam (for all the good it did me). Keep your meddling mouth shut while I threaten your mother or there'll be trouble …' He paused. 'Now then, where was I? Oh yes, marzipan fruits, that's right.' His expression darkened. 'But no raspberries. I can't even *look* at a raspberry these days – almond paste or otherwise,' he added with a shudder. 'Marzipan oranges, they're my favourite. I'd like twenty-three boxes of marzipan oranges, thirty-two pairs of trousers and a hundred pots of money. Big pots, obviously. I guess that'll do for starters.' He prodded the manuscript with his hook, jabbing a nasty hole straight through an unsuspecting letter 'T'. 'Come on then, what are you waiting for? Write me a proper story or else …'

'Or else what?' asked Mrs Hardluck-Smythe.

Captain Blunderfuss was surprisingly nimble for a man of his portly waistline, whirling round like a smelly spinning top in a blur of brown beard and flapping coat tails. Odelia didn't see the hook flashing through the air towards her until it was too late. Until it had already pierced through the collar of her last good dress, snaring her like a fish. She looked down in surprise (a *bad* surprise, not a good one) to find her feet dangling a clear six inches off the tea-splattered rug.

'Or else,' continued the pirate, with the meanest of brown-toothed smiles, 'the girl gets it.'

CHAPTER 3

A aarrgghhh!

Odelia's insides didn't take kindly to being dangled off the end of a pirate's hook. Her stomach came lurching up towards her throat, threatening to bring yesterday's toast with it, while her bladder developed sudden pressing needs of its own. The sight of the china-strewn rug swaying beneath her feet brought a dizzying rush of blood to Odelia's head, or maybe the blood was rushing in the other direction – it was hard to be certain. It was definitely rushing somewhere though, judging by her racing pulse and the black mist swooshing behind her eyes. There was a ringing buzz in her ears too – somewhere between a doorbell and a bee – but that was mercifully short-lived. And as the bee-bell faded away, a new noise filled her ears instead. A most unexpected noise indeed.

In other circumstances, the sound of her mother's laughter might have been something to treasure (it was the first time Odelia had heard her laugh since Father had gone). But the snort of merriment that came bubbling out of Mrs Hardluck-Smythe's nostrils hardly seemed appropriate to the snaring of her only daughter on the end of a pirate's hook. A scream would have been *much* more fitting. Because from where Odelia was standing (six inches off the floor with her legs crossed, trying to keep her panicked bladder in check), the situation was no laughing matter – quite the opposite in fact.

This can't be happening, said the rational, matter-of-fact part of Odelia's brain. *Everything about this is impossible.* Unfortunately, Odelia had stopped listening to the rational, matter-of-fact part of her brain round about the time a smelly, bloodthirsty pirate ripped through the collar of her last good dress with a wicked big hook. And besides, the impossibility of the situation – *a pirate? In Mayfair?* – didn't render it any less frightening. Odelia would certainly have been screaming, but the touch of cold steel against her cold neck seemed to have done something funny to her vocal cords. The best she could manage under the circumstances was a hoarse little whisper of a 'Help'. There was no one there *to* help though, that was the problem. Just her laughing mother and her giggling baby brother. And a fat lot of good either of them were.

Odelia's insides heaved as the pirate swung her from side to side like a pendulum. Like the heavy gold pendulum inside the backless grandfather clock, ticking down her last remaining moments until … until …

No! Please, no!

The last year of Odelia's life – those long, empty months she'd spent grieving for her beloved father – had been wretched. Watching Sammy grow had been the single ray of light in an otherwise gloomy and lonely existence. And yet now that her life hung in the balance – now that it was in danger of being snatched away by a disgruntled pirate with an inexplicable fondness for marzipan fruits and tailored trousers – Odelia discovered that she *was* rather attached to it after all. But it wasn't her life flashing before her eyes as she wriggled and squirmed like a hooked salmon on the end of a swinging line, it was her death.

She imagined walking the plank at sword-point – *that's what pirates do to their enemies, don't they?* – the wood wobbling beneath her feet with every teetering step. She imagined the cold rush of ocean air as she plummeted down to the angry waves below; the salt sting of the water as it rose up to meet her. And then (much against her better judgement) she found herself imagining the flesh-tearing teeth of circling sharks; picturing her last panicked splashes as they cut through the water to finish her off. What a horrible way to go.

But maybe she'd be lucky. Maybe Captain

Blunderfuss would set up a plank for her to walk right there, in the comfort of her own home. Levering up a loose floorboard would be easy enough with that horrid hook at his disposal and threading it out through the nursery window would be no trouble at all. And then … and then … No, there was nothing lucky about *that* ending either, Odelia realised. Shattered bones and spilt guts oozing down the pavement would be an even *worse* way to go. Not that it would come to that, of course, she reminded herself, trying to stay calm. Because Mrs Hardluck-Smythe would rewrite the story just like he wanted – of course, she would! – and then he'd *have* to release her.

'Help,' she whispered again, trying to spur her mother into action. It was no good though. Mrs Hardluck-Smythe refused to be spurred. 'Please, Mother,' begged Odelia hoarsely, as the effects of gravity took hold, tightening her collar round her neck and making it increasingly hard to breathe. 'Just give him what he wants.' Her vision was starting to blur now, the flower-patterned wallpaper and the dapple-grey hobby horse in the corner swimming before her eyes.

'Yes,' agreed Captain Blunderfuss. 'Give me what I want.'

'Absolutely not,' Mrs Hardluck-Smythe told him. 'I refuse to be dictated to by a figment of my imagination. And a filthy-looking figment at th–'

'*A pigfart of your imagination?*' interrupted the pirate. 'Who are you calling a pigfart?'

Mrs Hardluck-Smythe turned to Odelia and whispered, 'Don't worry, darling. None of this is real.'

Not real? The press of her collar against her throat certainly felt real enough to Odelia. She opened her mouth to argue, but any remaining words had already been squeezed out of her, along with her last lungful of breath.

Her mother had plenty of words left though. 'I said *figment*, not *pigfart*,' she told the pirate. 'As in, you're nothing but a figment of my imagination and you should get back to chapter fifteen where you belong. A chapter I'm increasingly behind with, thanks to this morning's rude interruption.'

'Rude interruption? I think she's talking about you,' hissed Captain Blunderfuss, swinging Odelia up to eyepatch level. 'Interrupting her work with your clumsy teapot smashing ...'

Odelia spluttered and gasped, an icy numbness creeping up from her feet.

'No, I'm not, I'm talking about *you*,' Mrs Hardluck-Smythe corrected him. 'You villainous varmint. *You're* the one interrupting me with your ridiculous demands for trousers. But it won't do, do you hear me?' She wagged a stern-looking finger in the pirate's face. 'Unhook my daughter at once.'

The pirate opened his mouth to protest but Mrs Hardluck-Smythe hadn't finished yet. 'Now,' she added with impressive firmness and authority.

Captain Blunderfuss let out a fish-scented snarl of irritation – *Harrumphh* – with top notes of unbrushed teeth and what smelt like a four-day-old lump of garlic wedged between his furry molars. But he did as he was told, setting Odelia back down on the rug and unspearing the collar of her last good dress.

Thank goodness.

'I'm not a varmint,' he said, sullenly, reaching down with his hook for a slice of fallen toast. He took a pirate-sized bite and chewed it thoughtfully. 'What *is* a varmint, anyway?'

CHAPTER 4

Unlike all the other questions buzzing round Odelia's brain – *Why did Mother dream up such a horrible character in the first place? How can he be a figment of her imagination if Sammy and I can see him too? Hasn't he noticed the rug fluff on that slice of toast he's eating?* – 'What is a varmint?' was one she could actually answer. Since her governess left, Odelia had been forced to take her continued education into her own hands. An education which mainly consisted of novels from the local lending library and the memorising of entire pages from her father's well-worn dictionary.

Another child might have begun at the letter 'A' and worked their way forwards through the alphabet. But the Earl Grey tea spots that ran from 'aardvark' down to 'abalone' were too painful a reminder of Mr Hardluck-Smythe – of his absent-minded dripping of tea-dunked biscuits over books and important paperwork – so Odelia had decided to learn the dictionary backwards instead. By the time she'd finally worked her way back to 'A', she'd be both older and wiser, and therefore better equipped to deal with any Earl Grey-inspired attacks of grief. That was the theory, anyway.

Dictionary digestion was proving a slow-going affair, however. Odelia had been lost in the vexatious verges of 'V' for weeks on end now, having only just reached such exciting entries as 'varicella', the technical name for chickenpox, and 'vagrant' and 'vagabond'. This meant that 'varmint' (an 'irritating or obnoxious person or animal') was still vitally, vividly – and indeed verily (an old word for 'truly') – fresh in her mind.

Which was why she was so surprised by her mother's alternative definition of the word …

'A varmint?' cut in Mrs Hardluck-Smythe, before Odelia could answer. 'A varmint's an unruly, *imaginary* character who terrorises young girls with their nasty great hooks and refuses to go back into their book where they belong. A varmint is someone who eats dirty toast off the floor and chews with their mouth open.'

Captain Blunderfuss opened his mouth even wider to protest (revealing an entire mouthful of soggy toast and rug fluff clinging to his brown-stained teeth) and then thought better of it. His jaws snapped shut again as he finished chewing.

'Heroes, on the other hand,' went on Mrs Hardluck-Smythe, '*always* return to their stories when they're asked to. Why, if Admiral Arbuckle had materialised behind the nursery curtains halfway through breakfast, he'd definitely be back in his book by now.'

The pirate glared, finishing off his toast with an impressively loud swallow, followed by an even louder belch. *Buuoooooeeerrrppp!* 'That's because Admiral

Arbuckle's a lickspittling nincompooper. And besides, no one's asked *me* nicely and kindly to go anywhere yet,' he pointed out, wiping his mouth on the back of his hook before reaching down for a second slice.

'Very well,' said Mrs Hardluck-Smythe. 'Would you, Captain Blunderfuss, do me the courtesy of returning to chapter fifteen so I can finish this book and send it off to Mr Pickfill? Please,' she added as an afterthought.

Odelia knew full well that the pirate's return to his book was the best solution for everyone. Captain Blunderfuss didn't belong in a crumbling house in London, he belonged on the seven seas (or seventeen seas, in his version), with his ship and his barrels of rum. And yet now that the immediate danger of plank-walking was past – now that she was safely unhooked, with both feet firmly on the floor and plenty of air back in her lungs – Odelia felt a surprising tinge of disappointment at the thought of the pirate's departure. What was it Father used to say? *Sometimes, Oddy, the most thrilling adventures are the ones right under our noses.*

There was certainly no doubting Captain Blunderfuss's ability to get under people's noses (which was why Odelia had taken to breathing through her mouth rather than her nostrils). He was smelly and uncouth, and his dental hygiene left a lot to be desired. As villainous varmints went, he was right up there with the best. But on the other hand, breakfast had never *been* so thrilling – not even when Father was alive. A pile of stale toast had never once turned into a hook-filled adventure before. And it had been a long time – a *very* long time indeed – since Odelia had seen her mother looking so vibrant. So vivacious.

'Hmm, let me think about that for a moment,' teased Captain Blunderfuss through another mouthful of toast. 'Do I want to be a good little pirate and get back into my book …? Nope. Are you *sure* you don't have any jam? What about marmalade?'

'We finished the last jar three months ago,' said Odelia. 'And before you ask, there's no honey either. Or butter. There's no *anything* any more.'

'What do you mean, "nope"?' asked Mrs Hardluck-

Smythe, refusing to be distracted by toast toppings.

'It's another word for "no",' said Odelia helpfully. She still had an awfully long way to go, dictionary-wise, until she reached the giddy heights of the letter 'N', but she already knew about 'nope'. It's what Nanny always used to say when Odelia asked her for extra pudding.

'Yes,' agreed the pirate with a gruff nod.

'Yes?' repeated Mrs Hardluck-Smythe, looking hopeful. 'As in yes you'll do as you're told and go back to your story?'

Captain Blunderfuss snorted so hard that something green and unpleasant flew out of his nose onto his toast. 'Why would I want to do that? I meant "yes", as in "yes, that's right, nope *does* mean no." ' He flicked the green unpleasantness onto the writing desk.

'But you have to,' insisted Mrs Hardluck-Smythe. 'If I don't get this book finished, then Mr Pickfill won't agree to publish it and we'll be forced on to the streets like penniless ...' She paused, searching for the right word. 'Like poor penniless ...'

'Vagrants?' suggested Odelia. 'Vagabonds?' 'V' was

turning out to be a very useful letter indeed, although neither word appealed very much. Life was bad enough already, without losing their home into the bargain. The thought of having to get a job in a match factory, where girls and women developed rotting jaws from the phosphorous, or ending up in the workhouse, sent shivers down her spine. *It won't really come to that though ... will it?*

'What if I don't *want* to go back to a life of storms and soggy sea biscuits?' said Captain Blunderfuss. 'What if I'd rather stay *here* and search for treasure instead?'

Odelia's eyes lit up like birthday candles. 'Treasure,' she repeated, savouring the word on her tongue. 'I could help you look for it and share the spoils!' Maybe Captain Blunderfuss was their ticket out of debt and destitution. The answer to all their prayers. 'Will there be priceless rubies and diamonds, do you think? Heavy wooden chests teeming with gold coins?' In her mind's eye she was already stacking the coins into neat countable piles. Already tipping them onto the counter at the grocer's shop in exchange for an entire cupboard's worth of jam. 'Have you got a map?' she asked, picturing a weather-worn affair, with tattered edges and the occasional blood splatter. 'Does X mark the spot? Oh please let him stay, Mother. Please.'

'Dada,' said Sammy, addressing a passing silverfish scuttling alongside his crib. Or maybe it wasn't the silverfish he was talking to at all. Because no sooner had the word left his baby lips than Samuel Rochester Hardluck-Smythe wrapped his chubby little fists round the bars of his cot and hauled himself upright, grunting and gurgling with the effort. 'Dada,' he said again, looking decidedly pleased with himself. His first foray into life on two legs obviously agreed with him. 'Piwate,' he added, pointing at Captain Blunderfuss. 'Dada piwate.'

'No Sammy, that's not your dada. *Your* dada is ...' Mrs Hardluck-Smythe couldn't quite bring herself to finish the sentence.

'Dada? Dada?'

Captain Blunderfuss's natural scowl softened,

the weathered wrinkles on his forehead smoothing themselves out like waves after a storm. And was that a tear he was wiping from his eye or just a stray toast crumb? 'Arrrr, hello there little feller,' he said. 'What's your name then? Do you want to help me look for treasure too?'

'Dada,' replied Sammy, somewhat predictably. 'Dada piwate.'

'You see?' said Odelia, clinging to the idea of treasure to keep her from thinking about their real dada. About the grey gloom of the cemetery with its moss-covered angels and slanting graves. 'Even Sammy wants him to stay. Please,' she begged.

'Hmm,' said Odelia's mother, starting to waver. Her command of the situation seemed to be slipping away again, as if the full impossibility of it all was finally catching up with her. 'I don't know. We've barely enough toast for the three of us as it is. And whatever will the neighbours say?'

Mr and Mrs Ponsonby-Smarm, their neighbours to the right, hadn't spoken to them in months. Not since

Odelia's green marble (the last ever gift from her father) had flown over the garden wall in an over-exuberant game of catch, smashing into their glasshouse. Maybe the arrival of a pirate was exactly what they needed to reopen the channels of communication. And maybe a neighbourly introduction to his hook would finally persuade them to return the marble. As for blind old Miss Batworthy on their left, Captain Blunderfuss could tar the entire house, with a skull and crossbones flying from every chimney, and she wouldn't notice.

'Think about your book,' said Odelia, hoping there *was* still a book to think about, now that the main character had (quite literally) jumped ship. 'Having a real-life pirate under your roof would be invaluable research. And if he *is* just a figment, like you said, then there's no harm in it anyway.'

Yes. It was working. Mrs Hardluck-Smythe was weakening by the second – Odelia could see it in her eyes.

'I'll be good, I swear,' said Captain Blunderfuss, dropping down onto his best knee. 'No stabbing people in their sleep, or weeing out the window. Pirates' honour.'

'Weeing out the window?' repeated Mrs Hardluck-Smythe, as if *that* was the part she found most troubling.

'Absolutely not,' promised Captain Blunderfuss. 'I'll stick to weeing in the pot plants like a proper gent. You have my word on that.'

Sammy chuckled, rattling the bars of his cot. 'Dada wee-wee!'

'But ... but ...,' protested Mrs Hardluck-Smythe, turning from the pirate to Odelia, to Sammy, with a defeated expression. 'I suppose if none of this is real, it doesn't matter *what* I say, does it?'

'Excellent!' Captain Blunderfuss beamed as if it was all decided. 'You won't regret it. This calls for more toast! You girl,' he said, clicking his fingers at Odelia. 'Fetch some fresh toast from the galley and quick about it. And something to wash it down with,' he added. 'The stronger the better.'

'This must be a dream,' said Mrs Hardluck-Smythe faintly. 'A strange, smelly sort of dream. In fact, a nightmare … that's the only explanation that makes any sense.' She laid her head down on the desk and closed her eyes. 'But when I wake up, this will all be over …'

CHAPTER 5

Odelia didn't go straight down to the galley as ordered. Not that Number 17 Hadlington Gardens even *had* a galley, on account of being a house rather than a ship. There were more pressing matters to attend to than toast-fetching. She headed for the bathroom, instead, to relieve her poor bladder, skimming through a story about local thieves as she tore a copy of the Mayfair Times into toilet paper strips, and then doubled back to her bedroom in search of a suitable treasure-hunting outfit. Whoever heard of a pirate digging up a chest of glittering rubies in a fraying flowery dress with a pink velvet trim? No one, that's who. And while the addition of a hulking great hole in the lace collar made it look *slightly* more adventurous than before, Odelia's dress was still far too fancy for a *proper* pirate.

A quick glance inside the doorless wardrobe (the doors having been sacrificed for firewood the previous month) suggested she might be out of luck when it came to finding a better alternative though. It wasn't that her clothes weren't old and raggedy enough, they were simply the wrong shape. A moth-eaten dress with a fraying hem was still a dress, and being a girl, Odelia had nothing *but* dresses at her disposal. Dresses, petticoats and bloomers.

Bloomers! 'That's it,' she cried, dashing across to the chest of drawers under the window. Odelia yanked open the top drawer and rummaged inside, tossing undergarments over her shoulder as she went.

'No. Not those ones, they're too clean … nope … nope … too white … too frilly … too ladylike … ah ha!' she cried at last, pulling out a nasty-looking grey pair, the colour of gathering rainclouds and factory smoke. Despite their dirty appearance, they were perfectly clean and sanitary – their unsavoury shading was the result of Odelia's own inexperience in the world of laundry. Her first-ever attempt at clothes-washing (the week after they'd waved a tearful goodbye to Hetty the maid) hadn't gone quite as well as she'd hoped. No one had told Odelia that whites and coloured clothes couldn't be soaked together, and she'd thought nothing of adding a rogue pair of black stockings and a passing pair of bloomers to a tub full of Sammy-soiled bottom-napkins. Luckily, Sammy was equally happy in grey bottom-napkins as he was in white (not that they stayed white for very long anyway) and Mother had been too wrapped up in her writing to care.

The grey bloomers, which were banished to the back of the drawer in dirty-looking disgrace, had probably given up hope of ever being worn again. But their moment had finally come. And what a moment it was – a glorious transformation from lowly *underwear* to the giddy heights of *overwear*. Odelia tugged them on over her proper bloomers to make grey pirate knickerbockers – ta-da! – and swapped her hook-holed dress for an old shirt of her father's to finish the look.

She'd smuggled the shirt out of Mr Hardluck-Smythe's laundry basket the night he died, hoping to hold on to the last traces of his snuff-and-kippers scent, cuddling up with it in the darkness like a comforter. Even when the smell had faded, she'd held on to the shirt with a fierce stubbornness, refusing to give it up when the rest of his clothes were sold. And while her father had never shown the slightest inclination to pick up a cutlass and sail the seven seas under a skull and crossbones, Odelia was sure he'd approve. This wasn't merely a dressing-up game of make-believe, this was a real-life treasure hunt to save her family from rack and ruin – from being turned out on the streets like vagabonds and vagrants and various other upsetting words beginning with 'V'.

Odelia fixed herself a makeshift belt out of one of Mother's black ribbons and clambered up on the bed to admire her outfit in the mirror, laughing out loud at the strange-looking creature reflected there.

'Aye aye, Captain,' she said, putting on her best pirate voice. 'Shiver me timbers and batten down the hatches – I smells treasure.'

That wasn't strictly true, of course. What Odelia *really* smelt was damp. Damp walls, damp ceiling and a damp patch on her bed where she'd knocked over a glass of water in the night. But who was to say what diamonds and rubies smelt like anyway? She unscrewed the loose metal rod from the end of her bed and returned to her position in front of the mirror.

'On guard!' she cried, wielding the metal rod like a sword. Yes, she was *really* starting to look like a pirate now. All she needed was a handkerchief for her hair, a black pirate patch (or maybe shutting one eye would do) and a big bushy beard like Captain Blunderfuss.

The beard proved surprisingly easy – soot from the fire mixed with generous helpings of spit made for a wonderful chin covering – but the handkerchief was a different matter. Odelia's were far too small and dainty to double up as a buccaneer's bandana. They wouldn't shiver a matchstick, let alone a timber. No, this was a job for a man's handkerchief, she realised, like the red-spotted ones her father used to blow his nose on. Big trumpeting elephant nose-blows they were, that wobbled his whiskers and left him red in the face (but with whistlingly clear nostrils).

It was funny, she'd forgotten quite how much she missed her father's elephant nose-blowing until now. Actually, it wasn't funny at all – for a moment there, it was heart-stoppingly, eye-wettingly sad. But only for a moment, because Odelia was a girl on a mission: a handkerchief-hunting, treasure-seeking, family-saving mission, which meant sadness would just have to wait. She dabbed at her eyes with her own, un-pirate-like lace hankie and tucked her feelings aside again, banishing them to the back of her mind for safekeeping.

'Anchors away!' she cried, hurrying off to her parents' bedroom (or 'Mother's room' as it was now called) in the hope that Mrs Hardluck-Smythe hadn't sold *all* of her husband's personal belongings yet. Suits and shirts were one thing, but handkerchiefs? Other than the rag-and-bone man, who hadn't ventured down Hadlington Gardens since Mrs Ponsonby-Smarm chased him with her spike-ended parasol, Odelia couldn't imagine anyone *paying* for a second-hand snot-catcher.

In some ways, the bedroom was barer than she remembered. Gone were her father's stern-looking wardrobe with the carved clawed feet and the squat chest of drawers under the window. Gone was the free-standing ebony mirror in the corner, with mother-of-pearl inlay flowers clustered round the glass. But in another way – a rather surprising, some might say *frightening* way – the bedroom was much *less* bare than Odelia had been expecting. She hadn't been expecting to find a flea-bitten, one-eared cat, stretched across the foot of Mrs Hardluck-Smythe's bed. And she *certainly* hadn't been expecting to find a flea-bitten, one-eared *pirate* snoring beside it, with his booted feet resting on Mrs Hardluck-Smythe's pillow. It looked like Captain Blunderfuss wasn't the only figment of her mother's imagination to have escaped out of her book.

'Ahh!' Odelia squealed in shock, before remembering that *she* was a pirate too now.

'Ah-haa!' she cried instead, pulling herself up tall and brandishing her bed rod at the sleeping intruders.

The cat woke up and hissed, its dirty white fir standing up on end as it glared at Odelia, but the one-eared pirate barely moved. 'Be quiet, Dog,' he murmured. 'I'm trying to sleep.'

Dog? Odelia looked around the room in confusion, but there was no dog. She checked under the bed. No, still no dog.

The pirate was snoring again now – snoring and dribbling into his short dark beard. At least Mother hadn't written *this* one with a hook, thought Odelia. At least he wasn't threatening to do her a mischief if he didn't get any velvet trousers and marzipan fruits. But the sight of his boots on Mrs Hardluck-Smythe's pillow was almost as worrying.

'Excuse me?' Odelia nudged his shoulder with the end of her bed rod. 'Would you mind taking your boots off my mother's pillow?' she asked politely. Just because she was sporting bloomers and a beard now didn't mean she'd forgotten her manners.

'Huh?' The pirate opened one eye and yawned a huge, cavernous yawn, offering an excellent view of his brown stubbed teeth and tonsils. 'Who are you? How did you get on board?'

'I'm Odelia,' said Odelia. 'I'm going to look for treasure with Captain Blunderfuss. But this isn't your ship, I'm afraid, it's Mother's bed, and she *won't* take kindly to having dirty pirate boots on her pillow. She's very particular about things like that.'

The pirate opened his other eye. 'My boots are perfectly clean, I'll have you know. I polished them with my own spit just this morning.'

'Hmm,' said Odelia. 'Between you and me, I'm not sure Mother's too keen on pirate-spit boots on her pillow either. Perhaps you could help me look for a handkerchief instead?'

'Or perhaps *you* can stop your pesky wiffle-waffling and let me get back to sleep,' suggested the pirate, 'before I ...' But the rest of his threat was lost to a fresh volley of snores.

Odelia gave up. The boots would have to stay for now. Maybe he'd take her more seriously once she'd found a handkerchief headscarf to complete her pirate outfit. She crept round the bed to her father's bedside cabinet, which had somehow escaped the great furniture sell-off, and opened the door. She half-expected to hear Mr Hardluck-Smythe's booming voice behind her, scolding her for her undaughterly nosiness – *Come now, Oddy. That's no way to carry on, is it? Snooping round in a gentleman's personal belongings?* But other than snores, and a loud piratical cry from the other side of the house – 'Nothing but toast? Why, the snivelling, snot-faced liar!' – everything was quiet.

Oh Father, she thought, as she peered inside. *Why did you have to leave us?*

If only Mr Hardluck-Smythe hadn't invested all their money in velvet knickerbocker shares, the week before the bottom fell out of the knickerbocker market. And if only he'd been *wearing* knickerbockers when he cycled back along the Thames path that fateful night, there'd have been no ankle hem to catch in the chain, catapulting him over the handlebars into the dark chill of the water … into the hard, unforgiving prow of a waiting coal barge. If only he'd stayed at home that evening instead, nursing his gentleman's cold with hot toddies and a plentiful supply of red-spotted handkerchiefs. If only.

There was a distinct lack of handkerchiefs of any colour at all on the top shelf. A distinct lack of *anything* come to that, save for a newspaper cutting about The Hose & Hope Knickerbocker Company's plummeting shares, and Mr Hardluck-Smythe's spare spectacles, which Odelia couldn't bring herself to touch. The bottom shelf, however, looked more promising. There was an old cigar box containing a lock of Odelia's baby hair, a tedious collection of postcards from Mr Hardluck-Smythe's late Aunt Ethel, and a commemorative Golden Jubilee biscuit tin filled with bow ties and cravats. It was three years since Queen Victoria's Golden Jubilee, but Odelia remembered it as if it were yesterday. Mr and Mrs Hardluck-Smythe had taken her to Buckingham Palace to watch the Queen setting off for Westminster Abbey. The cheering crowds were huge that day, and eight-year-old Odelia had been too short to see over everyone's heads, but Mr Hardluck-Smythe had lifted her up in his strong, fatherly arms, offering her the perfect view of the procession. A perfect view of the queen herself, no less, in her dress and bonnet, riding along in her open landau pulled by six beautiful cream horses, escorted by Indian cavalrymen and European princes.

Odelia pushed the Jubilee tin, and the memory of her father's arms, aside and carried on with her search. *Wait, what's that?* There, right at the very bottom of the pile, a red-spotted …

cravat.

Curses, thought Odelia. It must have escaped from the biscuit tin while no one was looking. And then she remembered she was supposed to be a pirate now, so she cursed again, out loud this time. 'Curses …' she cried, glaring at the offending cravat as if *it* was the source of all her troubles. As if the cravat was responsible for the fresh tears pricking at the corners of her eyes. 'Curses and custard!'

The cravat, rather like the teapot before it, said nothing. Odelia prised open the Golden Jubilee tin a second time, to reunite the cravat with its companions, but on a sudden whim emptied the whole lot out onto the bed beside the snoring pirate instead … just in case there were any stowaway handkerchiefs hiding at the bottom. There weren't. But what she *did* find was even more exciting. It was a small leather journal with the initials PAH-S embossed in gold across the front. *Father's diary!*

Odelia knew it was wrong to pry. She really did. And yet somehow her fingers were already turning back the cover, already tracing her father's careful handwriting across the inside leaf: *This journal is the private property of Percival Algernon Hardluck-Smythe. If found, please return to Number 17, Hadlington Gardens.* She could still see the determined glide and tilt of his pen working across the page. It was there in the neatly crossed 't's' and dotted 'i's'. It was there in that final flourish of ink on the 's' of 'Gardens'. It was like holding a piece of him in her hands ... and that was only the inside cover. *How much more of him will I find in the journal entries themselves?*

Just one tiny little peek, she told herself. *Just to see if there are any clues about where he kept his handkerchiefs ...*

CHAPTER 6

The first entry in her father's journal was a tedious account of fish-poaching – the tale of the stray cat who'd terrorised the Ponsonby-Smarms' ornamental carp the summer before last.

'Piddlesticks and poppycock,' said Odelia, who already knew how *that* story ended. Poor little pussy cat. 'Poop-cake and pudding rice,' she added for good measure, getting into the swing of cutthroat-cursing.

That little peek doesn't count, she decided, granting

herself one more. *Just one.* She turned to the final entry, dated 28th May – possibly the last words her father had ever written – and her next lot of curses wilted away to nothing on her tongue.

Calamity! she read. *Just received word from the accountant that my velvet knickerbocker shares are worthless. Beyond worthless. To think that I …* The rest of the sentence was too smudged to read, as if tears had mixed with the ink as he wrote. No, surely not. Odelia had never seen her father cry, not once. His stiff upper lip was as sturdy as the next man's. It must have been a sudden flurry of Earl Grey drips instead.

Oh misfortune, what have you done? What have I done? All our savings gone, just like that, the entry went on, *and the money I borrowed against the promise of promotion. How could I have been so foolish? So reckless? Instead of providing for my growing family in the years to come, I fear I have condemned them to a life of penny-pinching and shame. Ah, but who could have guessed there was no future in velvet knickerbockers, those finest of garments? What other trousers look as dashing teemed with a matching velvet waistcoat? What other clothing offers such an intoxicating sense of freedom around the calves?*

Alas. Knavish knickerbockers be damned! I rue the day I ever set foot (or leg) in their soft velvet trappings. Never, never, was a man brought so low by short trousers. If only I'd listened to my own natural caution instead of Mr Hose's honeyed promises of profit. If only I'd seen through his lies ... Oh wretched, wretched fool.

Where was Mr Hardluck-Smythe's stiff upper lip now? Odelia could scarcely believe such a wild outpouring of words had sprung from his pen. Maybe those smudges *were* the work of tears after all. She pictured her poor broken father weeping at his desk, his waxed moustache drooping with the weight of so much misery and guilt.

Enough of this despairing hand-wringing and blame-mongering. I must be strong for the sake of my family – for dear Constance and Odelia and the little one who's yet to make their way into the world. I must face my mistakes like a man and endeavour to find a path through these troubles. I must be grateful for what I <u>do</u> have, instead *of lamenting what is already gone. How can all be lost when I still have the greatest treasure in the world right here under my own roof? A treasure above all others, to be guarded with my very life. Yes, that is what I must focus on now. Perhaps a ride along the Thames will help clear my head and shift this wretched cold …*

Treasure? TREASURE? Why, that was exactly what had brought Odelia to the discovery of his journal in the first place! But her excitement was rudely pushed aside by her own tears. Thick, salty tears that stung her cheeks and dribbled out of her nose.

Don't do it, Odelia begged, clutching at the journal as if it could take her back through time to that fateful evening in May. *Don't clear your head with a bicycle ride. Stay here with us instead. Mother and I don't care about the lost money. We only care about you.*

'*There* you are, you miserable mop bucket,' came an angry growl. Captain Blunderfuss stood in the bedroom doorway, holding a dripping fish. A pretty orange and blue fish, with flapping fins and a round gaping mouth that snatched at the waterless air in big, thirsty gulps. 'I thought I told you to fetch me my rum. Some cabin boy *you* turned out to be.'

Odelia shut the notebook with a start, shoving it back into the biscuit tin with the bow ties and cravats, before kicking the whole lot under the bed. The last thing she wanted was horrid hook holes in her father's final words. 'Who are you talking to?' she asked, wiping her cheeks on the cuffs of Mr Hardluck-Smythe's shirt.

'I'm talking to you, you slippery slug-fart. I don't see any *other* runaway cabin boys round here.'

'What about him?' said Odelia, pointing to the snoring figure on the bed.

'Cook?' snorted Captain Blunderfuss. He didn't seem particularly surprised to see a pirate with his boots on the pillow. 'He's no cabin boy. He's not much of a cook either, come to that. All he does is sleep and burn things and let that mangy cat of his with the stupid name wee all over the deck.'

Odelia wondered what the cat's stupid name might be – *Whiskers McTiddlebum? Archibald Mouseface?* – but there was no time to ask. Cook gave a sudden start at the mention of his name and sat bolt upright. 'Ah, Captain, there you are,' he said. 'Me and Dog were just having a quick fifty winks. Did you want something?'

Aha! The cat's name is Dog, Odelia realised. *Yes, that is pretty stupid … not to mention confusing.*

'What I *want* is my rum,' roared Captain Blunderfuss. 'The rum I told my cabin boy to get,' he added, fixing Odelia with a one-eyed glare.

'You asked for more toast, not rum,' she pointed out. 'Toast and something to wash it down with. That's what you said.' He hadn't mentioned anything about making her his cabin boy, either, but Odelia kept that observation to herself. She rather liked the idea. She'd be like Jim Hawkins, the cabin boy in *Treasure Island*.

'Exactly,' agreed Captain Blunderfuss. 'Nothing washes down toast like a nip of rum. So where is it then? Where's my nip? A nip or a tot, I'm not fussy. I'll take the whole bottle.'

'We don't have any rum. It's water or nothing.' Odelia sniffed. 'What's that you've got there?' she asked, pointing at the fish. 'Where did you get it?'

Captain Blunderfuss shook his head in disgust. 'What's this?' he repeated, waving the poor creature around by its tail. 'It's a fish, you dribbling dunderhead, from that little pond over the wall.' He waved his hook in the general direction of the Ponsonby-Smarms' back garden. 'So much for there only being toast to eat! Turns out you're a fool *and* a liar.'

'You mean you stole it?' *Rats' tails and radishes! What will Mrs Ponsonby-Smarm have to say about that?*

'Course I didn't steal it,' said Captain Blunderfuss. 'Just because I'm a varmint, doesn't make me a thief. I caught this fish myself. Hooked it fairs and squares.'

'But you're not at sea any more,' Odelia reminded him. 'Land rules are different. Unless the pond belongs to you – which it clearly doesn't if you had to climb over the hedge to reach it – then it's still stealing. Put it back, quick, before the neighbours notice it's gone.'

'I'll do nothing of the sort,' spat the pirate. 'That's my breakfast you're talking about. Besides,' he added, giving the fish another shake. 'It's dead now, anyway.'

Odelia rather suspected he was right. It was certainly looking a lot limper than it had a few moments before. Maybe he was right about breakfast too … after all, a dead fish was no good to the Ponsonby-Smarms, was it? It would only upset them to find their prized carp floating on top of the water like a rotten egg, and if they happened to catch the pirate putting it back, there'd be trouble. Big trouble. Whereas if he gave the fish to Cook, to turn into a tasty grilled breakfast, they'd probably pin the blame on another stray cat instead.

'I *suppose* it's all right, just this once,' she agreed, putting on her strictest voice, 'seeing as it's already dead. But you're not to hook any more, do you hear me?'

The pirate said nothing. Odelia decided to take that as a 'yes'.

'And you have to share it,' she added, her stomach growling with anticipation. 'That's the other condition.'

'*Share?*' echoed Captain Blunderfuss. 'Why on earth would I want to do that?'

'Because …' Odelia thought for a moment, excitement

edging its way back into her brain alongside a generous helping of cunning. 'Because otherwise I won't tell you about the treasure,' she said. 'Father's treasure.'

CHAPTER 7

Any doubts Odelia may have had about teaming up with dangerous pirates vanished when Cook sliced open the fish and pulled out a round, slimy jewel.

'Shuddering shipwrecks!' cried Captain Blunderfuss, snatching it out of his hand. 'Looks like we've found the missing treasure already!'

Odelia stood on tiptoe for a closer look. *What is it?* A pearl? A ruby? An emerald? Yes, an emerald seemed most likely – there was a definite green tinge to it. How had it ended up in the neighbours' fish though?

Captain Blunderfuss rubbed it on his trousers and held it up to the light. It wasn't an emerald or a pearl or ruby. It wasn't any kind of jewel at all, but it *was* treasure. 'Pah!' he pahhed, tossing it onto the floor in disgust. 'Nothing but a lump of old glass.'

'My marble!' cried Odelia, scrabbling across the kitchen after it. She caught it, just as it was about to disappear under a cupboard, holding it up in triumph. Yes, it was definitely hers. She'd recognise that chip on the bottom anywhere. 'It's the one Father gave me when I was poorly with the chickenpox. With *varicella*, I mean. I was playing catch with it in the garden a few months ago, only I threw it too high and it flew over the wall into the neighbours' fancy new glasshouse. It must have rolled out of the door when they went to investigate and ended up in the pond. And then I suppose the fish must have mistaken it for his dinner.'

Odelia Harmony Hardluck-Smythe wasn't the sort of girl who went round kissing marbles. She wasn't the sort of girl who went round kissing *anything*.

But she was so overcome with relief at having it back safe and sound, that she found her lips puckering up for a welcome home kiss all the same. And then she remembered where her poor marble had been. Fish gut germs were bad enough, but nothing compared to the grizzly layers of grime encrusting Captain Blunderfuss's trousers. She gave the marble an extra wipe on her bloomer-knickerbockers instead and slipped it into her shirt pocket next to her fluttering heart. Today was turning out to be the most incredible day ever – a wild whirlwind of wonder and marvel – and she *still* hadn't even had breakfast!

'You know what that was, don't you?' she asked, patting her shirt pocket.

Captain Blunderfuss pulled a lump of wax out of his ear and rubbed it on the end of his boot, like shoe polish. 'Course I do. It's that bloomin' marble you've been wittering on about. Something to do with a grasshopper, wasn't it? I'd stopped listening, to be honest.'

'*Glasshouse*,' Odelia corrected him. 'Not *grasshopper*.

And it is a marble, yes, but it's much more than that too. It's a sign,' she declared. 'A sign from Father that he's watching over me and everything's going to be okay. A sign that he *wants* us to eat this fish for breakfast. That he wants me to find his treasure and save us all from rack and ruin.'

'More like a sign that one measly fish isn't enough,' said the captain, as Cook tossed the fish's head at a loudly purring Dog and started cooking. 'A sign that this father of yours wants us to catch some more …'

Oh no, thought Odelia. She already knew how *that* would play out – with Mrs Ponsonby-Smarm calling the police and Captain Blunderfuss and Cook getting carted off to jail. *And what if they arrest Mother too, for unleashing thieving pirates onto the streets of Mayfair? There's bound to be a law against that.*

'You're right,' she told him, thinking quickly. 'It's a sign we need to forget about the pond next door and head to Hyde Park instead. The Serpentine's teeming with fish.' Odelia crossed her fingers behind her back as she said it, hoping it would prove to be true. 'And we'll work out a proper treasure-hunting plan while we're there. How does that sound?'

Captain Blunderfuss grunted. But it was an agreeable sort of grunt that sounded more like 'Yes' than 'No'.

'Of course, the first part of the plan is finding the right treasure-hunting costume,' Odelia continued, feeling encouraged. 'And we've already covered that.' She gave an impromptu twirl, hoping to impress the pirate with her new outfit. She was particularly pleased with the addition of the toasting fork, which she'd tucked into her belt in place of the bed rod. The fork came with *three* sharpened prongs instead of just one. But Captain Blunderfuss couldn't have looked less impressed if he'd tried.

'Treasure-hunting's not a game,' he said gruffly. 'If it's dressing up and dancing you're after, you'd better find yourself another partner. Not that we *are* partners,' he added. 'Captains don't have partners, they have sub … sub …'

'Submarines?' suggested Odelia helpfully.

'Sub-ordinaries,' finished the pirate.

Odelia was pretty sure the word was sub*ordinate*, not sub-*ordinary*. It meant the same sort of thing as an inferior, or an underling. She didn't even need a dictionary for that one, she simply needed ears. It's what Mrs Ponsonby-Smarm always said (very loudly) when she'd finished shouting at the servants: 'If I say I want this fireplace scrubbed until it gleams then you'd better make sure it's gleaming, sprained wrist or no sprained wrist. Good grief, what did I do to deserve such insolent subordinates …?' But Odelia decided to keep her vocabulary corrections to herself, like the good subordinate she was.

'Yes, Captain,' she said, instead. 'No, Captain, I mean. I'm not here for the dressing up and dancing. I'm here for the treasure. I'll be the most extraordinary sub-ordinary you've ever had.'

'Good,' grunted the pirate, as Cook laid the freshly fried fish on the kitchen table and chopped it into pieces with his cutlass. 'In that case eat up and look lively.'

Mr and Mrs Ponsonby-Smarm's prized carp was a little on the charred side, but after all those endless months of dry toast it tasted like the finest food in London, if not the world. And if Captain Blunderfuss showed Odelia how to catch her own fish, maybe she could eat breakfast like this *every* day. With fish to spare for Mother and Sammy too, she promised herself, polishing off the last mouthful with a soft murmur of happiness.

'We'll have to do something with that hair of yours,' observed Captain Blunderfuss, as Odelia sat licking and re-licking her fingers. 'We don't want it getting in the way while we're fighting.'

'Fighting?' echoed Odelia, her daydream of daily fish feasts popping like a stray soap sud. 'Who are we going to be fighting?' Treasure-hunting was one thing, but vicious sword fights were a different matter. She didn't even *own* a sword. But then she remembered the marble in her pocket – her sign from Father that everything was going to be all right – and tried to think more courageously. She might not have a sword, but she *did* have a toasting fork.

'Treasure-hunting always ends with fighting,' said

Captain Blunderfuss matter-of-factly. 'It comes with the job. Unless you're too much of a lily-sliver?'

'Me?' said Odelia, forcing her shoulders back and treating him to her bravest, meanest stare. 'I don't even know what a lily-sliver is. If fighting's what it takes to find Father's treasure and save my family, then that's what I'll do. And if my hair's going to get in the way I'll—'

'Chop it off?' finished Captain Blunderfuss, reaching for Cook's fish-smeared cutlass. 'Exactly what I was thinking.'

The Ponsonby-Smarms' fish threatened to swim all the way back up Odelia's throat at the thought of the sharpened blade coming anywhere near her neck. 'N-no,' she stammered. 'Not chopping it off. I meant hiding it under a headscarf. That's what I was looking for upstairs.'

'A headscarf? I know just the thing.' Captain Blunderfuss hurried out of the kitchen, muttering something under his breath about grapes.

Grapes? What did grapes have to do with anything?

What if he meant the vine growing in the Ponsonby-Smarm's glasshouse? *Bedbugs and budgerigars,* Odelia cursed, setting off in hot pursuit. *Please tell me I'm wrong.*

She *was* wrong. Totally and utterly mistaken. It wasn't 'grapes' at all, it was 'drapes'. The dining room drapes, to be precise. Once upon a time they'd been her mother's pride and joy – the very latest in curtain fashion – but not any more. Not with her mother incapable of happiness *and* a large square of flowery material hacked out of the middle. The very same square of material currently residing on the end of Captain Blunderfuss's hook. He looked so pleased with himself though that Odelia didn't have the heart to say anything. At least, she didn't have the heart to say anything *bad.* What she actually said was, 'A headscarf! Why, thank you, Captain. That's perfect. I'll look like a proper pirate now.'

'A sub-ordinary pirate,' Captain Blunderfuss reminded her, in case she was getting ideas above her station. But he blinked his good eye as he said it, as if he was winking.

'Come on then, me hearty,' he roared, once Odelia was headscarfed up and ready to go. 'You too, Cook. Let's go catch ourselves some treasure. Batten down the hatshops and ankles away!'

CHAPTER 8

'Odelia?' called Mrs Hardluck-Smythe as the pirate crew headed for the front door. 'Is that you? I thought I heard voices.'

Odelia turned to see her mother coming down the stairs. *Darn and dung beetles. What will she say when she spots the hole in her curtains?*

'Oh ... er ... hello, Mother,' she stammered. 'We were just heading out for some fresh air.'

'You mean fresh fish,' Cook corrected her.

'The Certain Time is full of them,' added Captain Blunderfuss. 'That's what you said.'

Odelia suppressed a giggle. 'No, I said the *Serpentine* was full of them. We won't be long,' she assured her mother, who was staring from one pirate to the other with a look of sheer disbelief.

'Oh my,' said Mrs Hardluck-Smythe weakly. 'Now there are *two* of them. *Two* pirates from my book! I really *must* be dreaming. Yes, that's what you are,' she decided, pointing at the captain. 'A bad dream, not a figment of my imagination at all. A nightmare. I should have realised that when you started dangling my daughter off the end of your horrid hook.' She pinched her arm as if to wake herself up. 'No, it's no good, they're still there,' she muttered to herself. 'And Oddy's still wearing a bit of curtain round her head.'

'Oi,' growled the pirate, brandishing his hook. 'Who are you calling a nightmare?'

Mrs Hardluck-Smythe rubbed her eyes and blinked furiously. 'Or maybe I'm losing my marbles ...'

'Not you as well,' said Captain Blunderfuss. 'Have

you tried looking in next door's fish?'

Mrs Hardluck-Smythe blinked some more. 'Next … door's… fish?' she repeated weakly.

'In the pond next to the grasshopper … no, wait, that's not right.' The captain thought for a moment. 'Glasshouse, that's the one. There you go,' he said, turning to Odelia. 'Turns out I *was* listening after all.'

'Fish and grasshoppers? Oh my. This dream just keeps getting stranger …' said Mrs Hardluck-Smythe. 'And smellier,' she added, wrinkling up her nose.

'Right, that's it,' said Captain Blunderfuss. 'I've had enough of your rude insulks. Are *you* going to get rid of this whinging windbag,' he asked Odelia, 'or do I have to do it?'

Odelia leapt into action. 'No, that's fine, Captain. Leave that with me,' she said, taking hold of Mrs Hardluck-Smythe's arm and steering her back up the stairs. 'You're quite right, Mother, this is all a dream. And you know where the best place for dreaming is? Bed. You get back to bed and I'll take care of those pesky pirates for you.'

'And what about Sammy? Is he in this dream as well? I heard him calling for someone called Dada piwate wee-wee.'

'Don't worry, I'll take care of Sammy too,' Odelia promised. 'He can come with us to the park. A nice ride out in his perambulator will be good for him.'

'Yes,' said Mrs Hardluck-Smythe. 'Yes, he'll like that. And then when I wake up everything will be back to normal.'

Normal? I'm not so sure about that, thought Odelia. 'Things will certainly be better,' she agreed, stopping off at the nursery to collect her little brother. 'How many pirates *are* there in this book of yours, by the way?' It would be good to know how many more uninvited guests to expect.

'Only two at the moment,' said her mother. 'Captain Blunderfuss and Cook were the only ones who managed to escape Admiral Arbuckle. And the dog, of course. No wait, I just changed it to a cat, didn't I? For rat-catching purposes. I must remember to change its name too, otherwise it might be confusing for my readers.'

Very confusing, agreed Odelia, as she gathered a smiling Sammy up in her arms. She was pleased to hear that there were no more pirates on the way though. Two were more than enough to be getting on with.

'Dada!' gurgled Sammy. 'Dada piwate!'

'Oh, one more thing before I go ...' Odelia added. 'Did Father ever mention where he kept his gold and priceless jewels? A big chest, maybe, filled with rubies and diamonds?'

'Gold?' repeated her mother. 'Diamonds? Oh Oddy, your father didn't own any priceless jewels. If he did, we wouldn't be in this mess now, would we? He barely had a penny to his name when he died, thanks to Mr Hose and his empty promises of knickerbocker riches and glory.'

'But I saw ...' Odelia stopped herself just in time. The last thing she wanted to do was admit to snooping around in Father's private journal. And if Mrs Hardluck-Smythe really *didn't* know about her husband's secret hoard, then maybe it should stay that way. The less she knew about Odelia's treasure-hunting-fighting plans the better. That way she wouldn't try to stop her.

It was all very strange though. Why had Mr Hardluck-Smythe kept his hidden fortune a secret from his wife? Maybe it was for her own protection … maybe someone else was after the treasure too …

'Never mind,' said Odelia. 'You get back to bed and finish this dream in peace, Mother. I'll see you when you wake up.'

'When I wake up,' repeated Mrs Hardluck-Smythe. 'Yes. I look forward to that. No more pirates in the nursery. No more pirates in the hall. Just you, me and Sammy.'

'Exactly,' said Odelia, crossing her fingers behind her back. 'Sleep well,' she added blowing her mother a kiss. And when Mrs Hardluck-Smythe had gone, Odelia blew a raspberry on Sammy's fat little cheek to distract from the strange feelings jiggling round inside her – confusion and worry mixed with excitement and a touch of indigestion. Perhaps she shouldn't have eaten that fish so quickly. Or maybe this was what it felt like to be on the brink of an adventure, knowing that whatever happened, life would never be quite the same again.

If Odelia had known just how much hard work it would be taking two pirates, a baby and a one-eared cat called Dog to the park, she might have retired to bed too. She felt rather conspicuous walking through Mayfair in an old shirt and a pair of bloomers. A little chilly, too, truth be told. The fresh spring air champed at her bare knees, blowing her skin into purple goosebumps. But the cold was nothing compared to the chaos that seemed to follow Captain Blunderfuss wherever he went. A life on the seventeen seas had left him and Cook woefully unprepared for the bustling streets of London.

'A ship on wheels!' gasped the captain, pointing at a passing cab. The two ladies seated inside the passenger compartment looked equally surprised to see a one-legged pirate brandishing his hook at them.

'That's not a ship,' explained Odelia. 'It's a hansom cab. You tell the driver – that's the man who sits on the outside seat at the back – where you want to go, and he steers the horse in the right direction using the reins. And that one there, with four wheels, where the driver sits at the front – that's a brougham.' She was about to point out the horse-drawn omnibus coming the other way, crowded with passengers, when Captain Blunderfuss stepped into the middle of the road.

There was a volley of shouts and a wild whinnying of horses as he waved his hook at an approaching cab. 'Ahoy there!' he shouted. 'Take us to the Certain Time. We've fish to catch and treasure-hunting to plan.'

The startled driver pulled sharply on his reins and the passengers were thrown forwards in their seat.

'No, Captain!' cried Odelia, abandoning Sammy's perambulator and dragging Captain Blunderfuss back to the safety of the pavement. 'You'll get run over.'

'But you said I had to tell the handsome cabin man where I wanted to go, and he'd steer the horse for me.' He twisted his head back to growl at the driver. 'Not that he looks very handsome to me.'

'Nor me,' agreed Cook, who'd taken the opportunity for a quick lie down on the busy pavement.

Odelia tried not to laugh. 'It's a *hansom cab*, Captain, not a handsome cabin. And it's not for us, I'm afraid – we can't afford it. Besides, we can't leave Sammy and his perambulator, can we?'

'Dada piwate wee-wee,' Sammy said, kicking his legs in excitement as Dog pounced on a runaway leaf.

Captain Blunderfuss's expression softened. 'Aw, don't worry little feller,' he said. 'We won't be leaving you anywhere. You're one of the crew now.'

Odelia breathed a sigh of relief. 'Sorry,' she called to the furious-looking driver and passengers. 'You'll have to excuse the captain. He's still finding his land leg.'

'Dada piwate cwoo,' gurgled Sammy.

'That's right, Sammy,' said Odelia. 'And it's time this pirate crew set sail,' she added, grabbing hold of the perambulator handle again and pushing off along the pavement. 'Come on, you too, Cook. Before things get any crazier.'

Craziness seemed to follow Captain Blunderfuss wherever he went though. He upset a costermonger's barrow with an overexuberant wave of his hook, sending fruit and vegetables rolling off down the crowded street. He upset the feelings of a young dung-shoveller on Grosvenor Square, with a rude comment about the smell of his clothes. He even managed to get into a fight with a lamp post, that happened to be blocking his path. 'Out of my way, you scurvy scoundrel, or I'll shiver your timbers and scally your wags.' But after a slight detour up to Marble Arch, thanks to Dog chasing off after a rat, they finally reached the green open space of Hyde Park.

It was a relief to be clear of the noisy bustle and rush, to swap grimy roads and pavements for grass and trees. But Captain Blunderfuss was too busy grumbling on about marbles again to admire the scenery. 'If you're not throwing them at next door's grasshoppers and hiding them in fish, you're losing them altogether, like your weaselly word-witch of a mother. And now you're telling me that poncy big arch is made of marbles too?

Turnips and tommyrot. I know a big fat lie when I hears one …'

Odelia thought about explaining. She knew all about the history of Marble Arch from Father. She knew that it used to be the gateway to Buckingham Palace before it was moved, in time for the Great Exhibition of 1851. Father had told her all about the enormous crystal palace that had been built right there in Hyde Park for the exhibition too, displaying amazing marvels of the Victorian age from right across the world – everything from jewels and guns to pianos and kitchen appliances. But Captain Blunderfuss had already broken off from his moaning to do battle with a squirrel, so she decided to say nothing. Nothing apart from, 'Good work, Captain, that was a close one. You nearly had him there,' and 'Come on, the Serpentine's down this way. The sooner we find you your fish, the sooner we can start looking for that treasure.'

CHAPTER 9

Captain Blunderfuss seemed much more at home in the relative peace and quiet of Hyde Park. Not that it stayed quiet or peaceful for very long, once he and Cook started singing their sea shanties:

'Yo no no and a bottle of rum,
Watch out treasure chest here we come.
Silver and gold and diamonds galore –
No more toast off the tea-splashed floor ...'

Their terrible caterwauling was enough to scare off any squirrel within a two-mile radius, and any unfortunate passers-by who strayed within earshot were equally quick to make their escape. All save for the tall, elegant green-trousered gentleman with dark, beady eyes and a long, pointed nose, who seemed to positively *enjoy* having his ears scraped out by the sound of their singing. He followed them along the path, edging ever nearer as if he might join in at any moment.

'**Yo no no and a gallon of rum,**' sang the pirates, as Captain Blunderfuss jiggled Sammy's perambulator from side to side.

> '**Swishing all around in my pirate tum.**
> **Mouldy old biscuits and peaches of eight,**
> **And a parrot poo splat on my old tin plate.**'

'Gally wum! Poo spwat!' gurgled Sammy, beating his chubby fists against his blanket in time to the pirate's caterwauling. 'Dada piwate poo spwat!'

'Yo no no and a barrel of rum,
With a sunburnt nose and a sunburnt bum.
But down in the hold where it's dark and dank,
Scurvy old souls wait to walk the plank.'

'Do pirates *really* do that?' asked Odelia, watching the pointy-nosed gentleman out of the corner of her eye. Yes, he was still there. Still following them. He caught her looking and turned away to examine the late spring buds on a nearby shrub. 'Do you really make prisoners walk the plank?'

'Of course,' said Captain Blunderfuss. 'It comes with the job, like fighting and dirty underwear. 'Don't look so worried,' he added, mistaking Odelia's look of dirty-underwear disgust for one of concern. 'They always swim away to safety, more's the pity.' He let out a low snarl of disappointment. 'Rather a useless way of dealing with enemies now I come to think of it. I reckon that's your mother's fault – it must be. In fact, I wouldn't be surprised if that warbling old word-witch is behind *all* my problems.'

'I think you and Mother might have got off on the wrong foot,' said Odelia. She glanced down at the pirate's broom handle leg stump and blushed. *Oops. Bad choice of words.* 'I mean you got off to a bad start, that's all. She's really very nice once you get to know her. Honestly, she's the warmest, cuddliest, funniest mother in the whole world ... or at least, she used to be. I'm quite sure she didn't *mean* to chop off your leg and squirt poisonous squid ink in your eye.'

But Captain Blunderfuss wasn't listening. He was still brooding over his plank-walking problems. 'Thing is, I bind their hands up all mighty-tighty behind their backs, but somehow the rope always slips undone again before they hit the water. And there's never any circling sharks when you need them, neither. Admiral Arbuckle once got his toes nibbled by a passing seagull as he swam away but that doesn't count.' The pirate's face clouded over at the memory. 'That man's had more lucky escapes than I've had hot puddings. Not that I've had many of those lately. Cook doesn't do puddings, do you?'

Cook yawned. That seemed to be his answer to everything. Perhaps Mrs Hardluck-Smythe had used up all her best lines on Captain Blunderfuss. Or perhaps Cook was just naturally sleepy.

Captain Blunderfuss carried on regardless. 'A bit of fish and some mouldy old biscuit's as good as it gets on board *The Sea Lion's Bellybutton*.'

Odelia giggled. '*The Sea Lion's Bellybutton?* What kind of name is that?'

'Don't ask me,' snapped Captain Blunderfuss. He reached up his hook to a low-hanging branch as they passed and yanked it off. 'I wanted to call her *The Screaming Skeleton*, but somehow when I painted on the name it came out as *The Sea Lion's Bellybutton* instead. It must have been that meddling mother of yours again. Didn't want to upset her precious little readers … I've a good mind to–'

'What does he look like, this Admiral Arbuckle of yours?' Odelia asked, quickly changing the subject. They'd finally reached the Serpentine now. The water looked cold and murky – not the sort of place *she'd* choose to come swimming if she were a fish.

'Admiral Arbuckle?' The pirate wrinkled up his nose as if there was a bad smell in the air. 'Horribly tall and handsome and ridiculously elegant, worst luck. With a long, pointy nose and glittering dark eyes that can spot a pirate ship a nautical mile off. And as for his trousers …'

Odelia let out a gasp of recognition. 'He sounds exactly like the man who's been following us,' she said, dropping her voice to a whisper. 'Although I thought his eyes looked more beady than glittering. You don't suppose Admiral Arbuckle escaped from Mother's story too, do you?'

'What man? Where?' Captain Blunderfuss brandished his chopped-off branch like a sword.

'That man th–', began Odelia. But Mr Beady Eyes had disappeared. Their chosen stretch of the Serpentine was all but deserted, save for a smart-looking pair of green-trousered legs on a nearby bench. Presumably there was a face and body to go with the legs as well, but they were hidden behind the latest copy of *The Mayfair*

Times, with yet another front-page story about the gang of scurrilous thieves currently targeting the local area.

'He was right behind us,' said Odelia. 'I could have sworn he was. I thought he must be enjoying your singing.'

'Pah!' scoffed the pirate, swishing his branch against a nearby bush. 'It couldn't have been Admiral Arbuckle then. He *hates* my singing.'

'It's true,' piped up Cook, flopping down on the grass. 'He says it's like listening to a drowned cat with his tail caught in a scallop shell, which always upsets Dog.'

'Of course, *he's* got the voice of an angel, hasn't he?' grumbled Captain Blunderfuss. 'Bloomin' goodies and heroes, they're all too perfect for their own good.' He shook his head and sighed. 'It's not easy being a baddie, you know.'

'Dada? Dada badda?'

'Yes Sammy,' said Captain Blunderfuss, 'I'm afraid I am. But I'm not *all* bad. I once shared my last maggot-infested meal with a passing gull. That must count for something.' He dug around in his coat pocket and pulled out a scrunched-up wad of black netting. 'A *real* baddie would've shot the filthy feather-ball to pieces.' He unrolled the black netting and started looping it onto the end of his tree branch.

Odelia gasped again as she realised where the material had come from. 'What are you doing with Mother's mourning veil?' In truth, she hated seeing Mrs Hardluck-Smythe in her dark mourning clothes – her 'widow's weeds' as they were known – but that's what society expected of a grieving wife during her first year of widowhood. Or *every* year of widowhood in Queen Victoria's case. She still dressed in half-mourning clothes as a sign of her grief over Prince Albert, and he'd died in 1861.

'What, this old thing?' said Captain Blunderfuss with a mischievous grin. 'It's not a veil, it's a fish-catcher.'

'But … but …'

'Butterweed and bladder-snakes,' said the pirate, batting her objections away with a flick of his hook.

'Now what's all this about hidden treasure, eh? You promised you'd tell me while we were fishing.'

There was a loud rustle of newspaper from somewhere close by, followed by an even louder snore from Cook's mouth. He really was the sleepiest pirate Odelia had ever come across.

'There's not much to tell,' she said, watching with a mixture of horror and hope as the captain dragged Mrs Hardluck-Smythe's widow's veil through the water like an old wet dishcloth. Horror at what her mother was going to say when it came back covered in pondweed and fish scales, and hope that she might somehow return to her cheerful old self without it. 'All I know is what Father wrote in his journal – that the greatest treasure of all is right under our roof. He said he was going to guard it with his own life but then … but then …'

'Flibberting fart-hogs! No crying now,' said Captain Blunderfuss, pulling a squirming netful of silvery fish out of the lake and tipping them into the perambulator beside Sammy. 'There's enough salt water in the seventeen seas without it squirting out of your sub-ordinary eyeballs too. Here, give them a wipe with my hankie. Watch out for snot-droppings though.' He reached back into his coat pocket a second time as he spoke and pulled out a tattered scroll of parchment. 'Wait a minute, this ain't my hankie! It's ... it's a treasure map!'

He rested it on the hood of the perambulator, unrolling it to reveal a crudely drawn map, complete with an ink-splotted X slap bang in the middle. 'Blistering barnacle-bums! I don't believe it!' he cried, shaking with excitement.

'Festering ferret-feet!' agreed Odelia, trembling with anticipation.

'Golly McGosh with ribbons on it!' came a well-spoken exclamation from behind the newspaper. Whoever the mystery reader was, he was clearly enjoying the latest Mayfair news.

'Dada badda poo spwat,' added Sammy, not wanting to be left out. He gurgled happily as a wet fish flapped across his face, before grabbing it by the tail and throwing it down to Dog, who pounced on it hungrily. 'Spwat, spwat, spwat!'

'My first ever treasure map,' said Odelia, craning her head over the pirate's dandruff-encrusted shoulder. 'Where's it a map *of* though, that's the question? Is it a desert island from your book, do you think, or a real place, here in the real world?'

'Hmm. It certainly looks like an island. But I don't recognise any of these names …' Captain Blunderfuss jabbed his hook into the top left-hand corner of the map. 'See? I've never heard of Lake Hadlington. Or The Mayfairest Mountains.'

'But I have,' said Odelia, with a sudden flash of inspiration. 'At least I've heard of *Hadlington Gardens* – that's where my house is. In a part of London called *Mayfair*. And look there,' she told him, pointing at a long wiggly line running from one end of the island to another. 'The Ponsonby River. That's the name of our next-door neighbours, the Ponsonby-Smarms. The ones with the glasshouse and fishpond. And that forested area there – Batworth Woods – that must be named after our other neighbour, Miss Batworthy. Clothes moths and cutlasses!' she cried. 'I think it's all falling into place!'

Captain Blunderfuss held the map up to his good eye for closer inspection. 'So what you're saying is …'

'Yes,' said Odelia, her brain fizzing with excitement.

'That we're on a desert island?' finished the pirate, staring round with an air of bewilderment. 'It's not a very *warm* desert island, is it? Where are the palm trees? Where are the crabs? You know, those little red ones that pinch your toes when you're trying to have a paddle? In fact, where's the sea, come to that?'

'What? Of course we're not on an island. Well, I suppose we are really – this entire country is one big island – but that's not what I meant. What I was *going* to say was that Mother must have borrowed all the names of local landmarks when she was making your map. I think it's a sign.'

Captain Blunderfuss still looked confused. 'Like the marble, you mean? But how did it get into my pocket in the first place? It wasn't there yesterday – I'd have seen it.'

'Maybe Mother went back and added it into an earlier chapter while you were asleep. Anyway that's not the important bit. Look where the cross is. How perfect is that?'

'In the middle of a swamp?' The pirate grimaced. 'That doesn't sound too perfect to me. There might be alligators.'

'But it's not a *real* swamp,' said Odelia. 'Look at the name – PAHS SWAMP. P-A-H-S. Percival Algernon Hardluck-Smythe.'

Captain Blunderfuss still wasn't getting it.

'They're my father's initials,' she explained. 'Which means the treasure must be right there under our roof. At 17 Hadlington Gardens. Just like it said in Father's journal!'

There was another loud rustle of newspaper from the nearby bench, but Odelia scarcely noticed. Her head was too full of diamonds and pearls and big clunking gold coins. It was too full of warm new clothes and dinner plates piled high with cakes and cucumber sandwiches. 'Mother said she didn't know anything about hidden jewels, but she *must* have done. This *proves* it. Why would she lie though?' Odelia wondered out loud. 'Maybe she's already tried looking for the treasure, but it's too well hidden. Maybe she didn't want me getting my hopes up.'

'Or maybe she's already squandered the family fortune on velvet trousers and marzipan fruit,' suggested Captain Blunderfuss, scowling at the very thought. 'I wouldn't put it past her, the miserable old maggot.'

'No, Mother would never do that. She doesn't even *wear* trousers. Come on,' said Odelia, 'we've got what we came for. The fish, I mean. Let's get back and look for that treasure.'

'Aye aye, Sub-ordinary. Ankles away!' Captain Blunderfuss grinned as he stuffed the map into his pocket. 'Wake up, you lazy lumpfish,' he told Cook, nudging him with his broomstick leg. 'We're off to find us some treasure.'

'Spwat, spwat, spwat,' said Sammy, tossing the last of the wriggling fish down to Dog as Captain Blunderfuss swiftly swung the perambulator round in a circle, heading for home.

CHAPTER 10

BREEEEEEEP! The pirate crew had just reached the edge of the park when they heard a shrill whistle. A *police* whistle.

Odelia's chest tightened. Mr and Mrs Ponsonby-Smarm must have sent them to arrest Captain Blunderfuss for stealing their prized carp. Or maybe someone – the gentleman with the newspaper, perhaps? – had reported him for fishing with a widow's mourning veil. There was bound to be a law against that. Either way, they needed to make their escape, fast. That was easier said than done though, with Captain Blunderfuss chasing after a pigeon who'd made the mistake of pooing on his pirate hat. Cook, meanwhile, had taken the opportunity for another catnap on a nearby bench, and Dog was busy being sick under a rose bush after eating too many fish.

'Captain,' hissed Odelia. 'We need to go. *Now.*'

But Captain Blunderfuss was still shaking his hook at the pigeon. 'Come down from that tree, you scurvy scoundrel, and fight me like a man. A grey, feathery-winged man with silly pink feet.'

'Coo,' said the pigeon. 'Coo, coo, coo.'

'Don't you coo me, you rabid rascal …'

BREEEEP!

Odelia tugged at the captain's coat. 'Hurry, I *mean* it,' she begged. She couldn't afford to lose Captain Blunderfuss now. Not with so much at stake. It wasn't just the map in his pocket she'd miss if he got carted off to prison, or his treasure-hunting expertise. It was *him*, Odelia realised. He might be a rude, smelly criminal with an unfortunate habit of hooking people by the collars, but she'd grown surprisingly fond of him during their brief time together. The thought of going back to her lonely fatherless existence without him made her feel hot and panicky inside.

BREEEEEEEEEP! **BREEEEEEP!!** The police whistle was growing louder and closer with every blow.

'Quick,' Odelia said, changing tactics and steering the captain into a nearby clump of bushes. 'Hide in there, and don't come out until I say so, otherwise …' *Otherwise what?* What would be bad enough to scare an unruly pirate like Captain Blunderfuss into doing what he was told? 'Otherwise there'll be no velvet knickerbockers waiting for you when you get home.'

'Velvet knickerbockers, did you say?'

'Yes,' said Odelia, crossing her fingers behind her back. She didn't like lying, but this was an emergency. 'I found some of Father's old ones this morning. You'd be welcome to have those. Only if you stay there though. Stay down and stay quiet.'

Captain Blunderfuss disappeared out of sight, just

as the whistle-blowing policeman came *into* sight.

'And stay still,' Odelia whispered as an afterthought. 'I'm going to take a leaf out of Mother's book and pretend you're not here.'

'You can take this leaf out of my nostril while you're at it,' came the less-than-quiet reply. 'This bush is itchier than a hammock of bedbugs.'

'Shhh,' shushed Odelia. 'Unless you want to end up in jail, stop talking. I mean it. Ah h-hello there, Constable,' she stammered, as a red-faced policeman with an enormous moustache came to a panting halt beside her.

'Sergeant,' the policeman corrected her. 'Sergeant ... Thataway.'

'Sorry Sergeant,' said Odelia. 'L-lovely morning, isn't it? Or do I mean afternoon?' In truth, it had been such a peculiar day she'd lost all track of time. The making of the morning toast seemed to belong to another lifetime altogether.

'No ... time ... for idle ... pleasantries ... and small talk,' said Sergeant Thataway, struggling to regain his breath. 'Not with a fearsome criminal … on the loose. A vile varmint of the lowest order.'

'A fearsome criminal? A varmint?' Odelia tried her best to look surprised, even while the little voice in her head was thinking: *Flapjacks and fruit flies, it's all over now. The game's up.* 'I can't help you there, I'm afraid. I haven't seen any varmints round here.'

There was a loud rustle behind her. 'Stop tickling my nose, you lily-slivered leaf or *you'll* be walking the plank too.'

Sergeant Thataway frowned. 'What was that?'

'What was what?' asked Odelia innocently. 'I didn't hear anything. Just some birds in the bushes that's all. I think they've got a nest in there.'

The policeman's face lit up. 'Ooh lovely,' he said. 'Perhaps it's blackbirds. They're my favourite. I might have a little peek while I'm here.'

'No!' cried Odelia. 'It's er … it's definitely not blackbirds. It's erm …' She racked her brains, trying to think of something less attractive. Wasps? Rats? '*Vultures*,' she finished. She'd never actually seen a vulture, but she'd read about them in the 'V' section of Father's dictionary, and they sounded like pretty unpleasant creatures.

'Vultures? I wouldn't have thought so. Let *me* see …'

'No!' cried Odelia a second time. 'Not vultures, I meant … Ooh look, there he is now!' She pointed in the opposite direction, away from Captain Blunderfuss's hiding place and away from Cook's bench. 'The pirate,' she added, as Sergeant Thataway spun round to see. 'He went that way, Sergeant, I just saw him now. If you're quick, you should still be able to catch him.'

But the policemen refused to take the bait. His eyes narrowed. 'Vultures?' he repeated. 'Pirates? Do I *look* like a fool to you? I've a good mind to take you in for wasting police time.'

Odelia had never been so confused. 'You mean you're *not* looking for a pirate? I thought you said there was a fearsome criminal on the loose? "A vile varmint", you said.'

'Yes,' said Sergeant Thataway, with a sigh of exasperation. 'Exactly. The head of the Mayfair Mob

– the gang of thieves behind a series of local robberies. We received reports of a man matching his description right here in the park. Tall, handsome and elegant, by all accounts, with a long, pointy nose, dark glittering eyes and a fine line in velvet trousers. Looks a proper gentleman, he does, and sounds like one too. But don't let that fool you. He's a varmint all right, and no mistake.'

Odelia gasped out loud in a mixture of relief and shock: relief that it wasn't Captain Blunderfuss the police were after, and shock that the varmint in question sounded *exactly* like the green-trousered gentleman who'd been following them earlier.

Odelia wasn't the only one reeling from the revelation, either.

'That sounds like Admirable Arbuckle!' exclaimed the bush. 'That drivelling, do-gooding dung face.'

'Oi. Who are you calling a dung face?' demanded the policeman, treating Odelia to a long hard stare. 'And why's your voice gone so low and growly all of a sudden?'

Odelia responded with a burst of theatrical coughing. 'Sorry Sergeant,' she spluttered. 'It must have been a frog in my throat.' She finished off with a croak or two for good measure. 'I was talking about the er … that dreadful varmint you're looking for. What a dreadful dung face! I do hope you catch him.'

She coughed again as the bush let out a string of furious curses. 'Oh no, you don't,' it growled, its leaves shaking with agitation. 'That's *my* job. I've been waiting fifteen whole chapters to wipe the smile off his smug elegant face. If anyone's feeding him to the sharks, it's me.'

'Dear, oh dear. You want to see a doctor about that nasty chest of yours,' said Sergeant Thataway, more kindly. 'Before it gets any worse. That sounds suspiciously like the cough that carried off my father, God rest his soul.'

Odelia nodded. 'Yes, Sergeant. I will. Thank you.' Her voice really *was* growly now. All that coughing and spluttering had given her a terrible sore throat. 'This thief of yours,' she added. 'What colour were his trousers?'

'Green,' confirmed the policeman.

Odelia nodded. Yes, that sounded *exactly* like the man she'd seen earlier. She could still picture his trousers quite clearly … smartly tailored ones in a rich, vibrant shade, midway between lime green and bottle green. The exact same shade of trousers, now she came to think about it, as the man sitting on the bench by the lake had been wearing. The man with his face hidden behind his newspaper. What if they were one and the same person? What if he really *had* been following them, then picked up a discarded newspaper from the bench and hidden behind it to listen in on their conversation? A conversation all about hidden pirate treasure … Odelia felt queasy all of a sudden as she remembered the part where she'd announced that the treasure must be hidden at 17 Hadlington Gardens …

Curses and cauliflower ears! How could she have been so careless? The villain might be at the house already, hunting for the missing treasure, while they were busy fighting pigeons and chatting to policemen in the park. He could be making off with Father's precious rubies and gold at that very moment, taking Odelia's last chance at saving her family's fortunes with him.

She weighed up telling Sergeant Thataway. Maybe it wasn't too late. Maybe they could still catch the villain in the act if they hurried. *But what if Mrs Ponsonby-Smarm reports Captain Blunderfuss for stealing her fish while we're there?* If the police weren't after a pirate *now*, they soon would be.

'*Green trousers?*' Odelia repeated. 'Yes, that sounds like the fellow I saw. Your villainous varmint, I mean. Not the pirate. I haven't seen any of those around here, I'm afraid. Not a single one. Although if I had, they'd definitely have gone that way too.'

It was a rather anxious, jittery sub-ordinary who led the pirates and the perambulator back through the elegant streets of Mayfair to 17 Hadlington Gardens. But there was no sign of any breaking and entering when they reached the house, much to Odelia's relief. No sign of any ransacking or robbery; of the house having been turned upside down in search of Mr Hardluck-Smythe's elusive hoard. The front door was still firmly on its hinges and all the windows seemed intact. But if it really *had* been the leader of the Mayfair Mob listening in on their treasure map conversation in the park, it was only a matter of time before he and his criminal crew came looking for Father's hidden hoard. The sooner Odelia found it and moved it somewhere safe, the better.

She opened the front door to find a black-edged business card from 'Waterloo Woodworm Treatment Services' waiting on the doormat. A black-edged business card with a spidery handwritten note scrawled on the back:

We have reason to believe that the structural integrity of your house may be at risk due to a particularly virulent strain of woodworm operating in the area. We would recommend a no-obligation examination of your interior at your earliest convenience – a member of our highly specialised team will call back later to discuss a suitable time.

Hmmm. The idea of a complete stranger offering to poke round their house for them, so soon after Odelia had broadcast news of her hidden treasure, seemed more than a mere coincidence. *Much* more. Her hands were shaking as she passed the card on to the pirate. But he didn't seem remotely worried about pest control impersonators or the integrity of the house.

'Integrity?' he snorted dismissively. 'I don't even know what that is. Sounds like a scurvy excuse to keep me from those velvet knickerbockers you promised me. Enough with the worry-warting, Sub-ordinary, it's trouser time!'

Odelia was still worrying as she followed the captain down the hall. She was worrying what he'd say when he realised there weren't any velvet knickerbockers waiting for him. She was worried what Mother would say when she discovered Sammy was covered in slimy fish scales. And she was still worrying about the Waterloo Woodworm Treatment Services. Captain Blunderfuss might have dismissed it, but there was something very suspicious about that card. It felt like ... like a net closing in on them. Not a homemade fishing net this time though. A tight net of criminal trickery and guile. She'd just have to hope she was wrong.

CHAPTER 11

'There you are, Oddy,' called Mrs Hardluck-Smythe, emerging from the kitchen as Captain Blunderfuss and Cook disappeared upstairs in search of the promised knickerbockers. 'I've been looking *everywhere* for you.'

'Mother!' Odelia hid the black-edged business card behind her back, before Mrs Hardluck-Smythe got any ideas about inviting suspicious-seeming woodworm specialists to poke around the house. 'I thought you were in bed.'

'Mama!' echoed Sammy, kicking his feet with excitement. 'Mama bed-bed!'

'Yes, I *was*,' said Mrs Hardluck-Smythe, 'but I couldn't stay there. I had to get up and start writing. I had the most marvellous dream about my pirate, you see. The one from my book. It was so real. He was right there in the nursery, demanding jam, for some strange reason – I forget now. Jam, trousers and marzipan fruits. Yes, that's right. And you and Sammy were there, too, as real as anything, with Sammy calling for his dada and you dangling off the end of the pirate's hook like a flappy little fish.'

'Dada piwate spwat spwat!'

'It wasn't a very nice dream, obviously,' Mrs Hardluck-Smythe continued, 'but it's worked wonders for my characterisation. My pirate captain's really starting to come to life now. After weeks of struggling to find the right words, his voice has been coming through as clear as a bell.'

A bell? thought Odelia. *More like a foghorn.*

'The book's going so well, in fact, that I've decided to give myself the afternoon off and spend it with you and Sammy. I thought we could visit the Natural History Museum.' Mrs Hardluck-Smythe paused, as if she was waiting for a response – for a *How lovely, Mother, what a wonderful idea.* But the *how lovely* never came. Odelia was too busy panicking for that.

The promise of an afternoon outing would normally have been something to look forward to. A rare gem of proper family time to treasure. But Odelia had other, more urgent, treasure on her mind right now. She *had* to find Father's loot before the Mayfair Mob came looking for it. There were no two ways about it. How was she supposed to do that if she was trudging round a museum though? And what about Captain Blunderfuss and Cook? The thought of leaving two unruly pirates alone in the house for the afternoon, while Odelia played happy families with Mother and Sammy, was a very worrying thought indeed.

She was just about to make up an excuse – a headache perhaps, or a tummy ache from eating too much toast – when there was an almighty thump from upstairs, followed by a volley of curses.

'Good heavens,' gasped Mrs Hardluck-Smythe. 'Whatever was that? It almost sounded like …'

'A bat!' said Odelia, blocking her path to the stairs. The sight of Captain Blunderfuss ransacking Father's few remaining belongings in search of a pair of velvet knickerbockers would be too much for her poor mother. There'd be no writing *that* off as a dream. The treasure-hunting would have to wait, after all. 'I mean a rat,' she corrected herself. 'I mean a … yes, let's go to the Natural History Museum. Let's go straight away. How lovely. What a wonderful idea. You'd like that too, wouldn't you, Sammy? You'd like to go and see the animals with Mother and Oddy?'

'Mama Oddy anmoos,' agreed Sammy, waving his fishy little fists in the air.

It was a long, weary trudge to the museum, back across

the corner of Hyde Park, down through Knightsbridge and on into South Kensington. Odelia tried to cheer herself up by thinking how different their lives would be when she tracked down her father's hidden hoard. *We won't have to walk everywhere for one thing.* Her mind drifted to the new underground electric railway being built deep under the city – *how exciting!* – and to steam train trips to the seaside.

She found herself thinking nostalgically about the family holiday to Lyme Regis a few years before, when Mr Hardluck-Smythe had taken her fossil hunting. Odelia had pretended she was Mary Anning, the famous fossil hunter and palaeontologist, looking for a plesiosaurus, and her grandmother had fainted clean away at the thought of a dinosaur on the beach. Luckily Mrs Hardluck-Smythe had been on hand with her smelling salts to revive her. There'd been no dinosaurs to discover that day though, just fellow holidaymakers, horse-drawn bathing machines and a strong briny breeze that had whipped her mother's hat clean off her head as they strolled along the Cobb before dinner.

It was a warm, happy kind of memory, but a sad one too. Odelia's grandmother had died the year before her father, carried off by a nasty bout of pneumonia. And now Mother and Sammy were the only family Odelia had left, and they could barely afford to eat, let alone take a train to the seaside. Even bumpy rides along the cobbled streets in a hansom cab or a brougham seemed like a dream luxury these days.

The memory of Captain Blunderfuss's brush with the 'handsome cabin' led Odelia straight back to thoughts of the chaos she'd left behind at 17 Hadlington Gardens: two pirates in search of non-existent knickerbockers, one vomiting cat, a missing fish from the neighbours' pond, a highly suspicious-seeming woodworm specialist threatening to call again and the possibility of a gang of local thieves plotting to steal the family treasure before she'd even had a chance to look for it.

She tried not to let her worry and frustration show, however. It was their first family outing in a very long time, and it was nice to see Mother getting some proper fresh air. Mrs Hardluck-Smythe had even forgotten to change into her full mourning outfit, which was a promising sign (and something of a relief given the fishy state of her black veil). She seemed almost like her old self as she chattered away to Sammy about all the different animals and exciting fossils they'd see when they got there.

Odelia had always enjoyed the museum's exhibits, but it was the building itself she loved best of all. She liked the huge, cathedral-like central hall, with its grand staircases and impressive curved roof, and the statue of Mr Darwin in gleaming white marble. She liked the animal carvings peering out from pillars and arches. And she particularly liked the beautiful ceiling panels high above her head, painted with pictures of plants. They were always Mr Hardluck-Smythe's favourite too. He even used to bring his opera glasses with him in order to study them more closely. And it was that thought – the memory of her father's snuff-scented hand in hers as they leant out over the upper balcony for a closer view of the ceiling – that made Odelia determined to put aside her worries and enjoy herself. Or at least *pretend* to enjoy herself for Sammy's sake. He might not have a mother and a father to share these things with, but he *had* a mother and a big sister and that was something.

The afternoon really *was* enjoyable … right up to the moment when an opinionated lady in a high-necked, ruffled day gown took it upon herself to lecture Mrs Hardluck-Smythe about the state of Odelia's dress. Or rather the *lack* of Odelia's dress.

'They're not bloomers,' said Odelia defiantly. 'They're knickerbockers. And it's not a piece of curtain, it's a headband.'

The lady looked down her nose at Odelia as if she was something unpleasant on the heel of her lace-up leather boot. 'Children,' she said, 'should be seen and not heard. Although given the state of your attire, I think it might be better if you weren't seen either.'

'Excuse me! How my daughter chooses to clothe herself is not a matter for public debate,' said Mrs Hardluck-Smythe. 'So I'll thank you to keep your small-minded opinions to yourself, you trumped-up turnip-face.' It was a glorious moment – a moment which sent the lady in the ruffled gown reeling back in horror (looking more ruffled than ever) and had Mrs Hardluck-Smythe covering her mouth with her hand, as if she couldn't quite believe what she'd said.

Once the moment was over, the spell was broken though. Sammy took the opportunity to refill his bottom-napkin, and Mrs Hardluck-Smythe started sobbing about how writing her pirate book was turning *her* into a pirate too. Then she moved on to sobbing about neglecting her children, and knickerbockers, and how much she missed Mr Hardluck-Smythe. She cried so hard that she soaked right through her pretty lace handkerchief and Odelia had to lend her the curtain headband to blow her nose on.

'Thank you, Oddy,' said her mother. 'I'm sorry for causing such a scene. I don't know how much longer I can keep on like this. What if my book's no good? What if Mr Pickfill refuses to buy it, and we're forced on to the streets like penniless …' She paused, searching for the right word. 'Like poor penniless …'

'Vagrants?' suggested Odelia, just as she had that morning. 'Vagabonds?'

Mrs Hardluck-Smythe blinked in surprise. 'Do you know?' she said with a sniff. 'Those are the exact same words as were in my dream. Yes, it's all coming back to me now. I was trying to persuade my pirate – Captain Blunderfuss – to return to his book, saying I had to get it finished otherwise we'd be forced on to the streets like penniless … and then you said …'

'I know,' said Odelia. 'I was there.' It felt wrong keeping up the lie with her mother so upset. 'It wasn't a dream. He really *did* escape out of his book. He really *did* hang me off the end of his hook. And you said he could stay if he promised not to stab people in their sleep or wee out the window. He's not a dream, and he's not a figment of your imagination. He's as real as you and me. And Cook. *And* Dog the cat. They must have escaped out of your book too.'

Mrs Hardluck-Smythe looked dazed.

'I know it's a lot to take in but it's true. And

they're going to help us find the missing treasure and everything will be all right. You'll see.'

'But … but …'

'Butterweed and bladder-snakes,' said Odelia, reaching up on tiptoe to kiss her mother's chin. 'Let's go back home, and I'll introduce you properly.' *Assuming we've still got a home*, she added silently, wondering how 17 Hadlington Gardens had fared with Captain Blunderfuss in charge.

CHAPTER 12

The house was still standing – that was a good start. And the pirates were still in residence. Odelia could hear Captain Blunderfuss's singing from halfway down the street:

'Captain Me had a fine treasure chest,
Bigger and better than all the rest.
Filled with treasure so shiny and new,
In black and mauve and peacock blue.

Yo, ho, ho, what fine, fancy legs,
Perfect for pirates with broomstick pegs.
The Admiral's face will be green as grass
When he sees them clinging to my pirate–

Jiggling jellyfish!' he broke off, at the same time as Odelia, Sammy and Mrs Hardluck-Smythe headed up the neglected and overgrown front path. 'Is that gold piping? These are even better than that trumped-up treacle-snot Admiral Arbuckle's. My legs and broom handle will be the toast of the seventeen seas in these.'

'It certainly *sounds* like my pirate,' said Mrs Hardluck-Smythe. 'And I'm definitely not dreaming this time?'

'Definitely not,' Odelia reassured her, opening the front door.

'Ah-ha! *There* you are, Sub-ordinary!' cried Captain Blunderfuss, barrelling down the hall in a pair of black velvet knickerbockers with fancy gold piping. 'I found my trousers! They wasn't buried, like I thought they would be though. They were up in the crow's nest.'

Sammy cooed with delight as the pirate bent down to tickle his tummy. 'Dada! Dada piwate!'

What trousers? thought Odelia, staring at Captain Blunderfuss in surprise. *What crow's nest? Does he mean the lookout platform on a ship?*

Odelia wasn't the only one who was surprised. 'It's true,' gasped Mrs Hardluck-Smythe. 'You're really here. And you're not just a figment of my imagination?' She reached out her finger and prodded the pirate in the chest.

'Enough with the pigfarts!' roared Captain Blunderfuss. 'I ain't no more pigfarty than you are, you putrid old pigeon-bum.'

Mrs Hardluck-Smythe let out a merry tinkle of laughter. 'Putrid old pigeon-bum? Ha! Do you mind if I pinch that for my book?'

'I certainly *do* mind,' said the captain. 'No one pinches *my* putrid pigeon-bum, thank you very much.'

'Dada piwate bum bum!' gurgled Sammy. 'Cookie cat-cat!' he added as Cook arrived on the scene, sporting a pair of mauve velvet knickerbockers, with

Dog cradled in his arms.

'I still don't understand where the knickerbockers came from,' said Odelia. 'Was that you, Mother? Did you write them into your book while we were out at the park?'

'*She* didn't do nothing,' said Captain Blunderfuss crossly. '*I'm* the one that found them. A whole trunk of them there were, up in the crow's nest, like I told you.'

'But we don't *have* a crow's nest.'

The captain looked at Odelia as if she was stupid. 'You know, the *up*-upstairs bit, with all the dust and the spiders.'

'You mean the attic!' said Odelia. 'I wonder how they got up there.'

Mrs Hardluck-Smythe wasn't laughing any more. 'They were your father's Hose & Hope knickerbockers,' she said quietly. 'He must have hidden them up in the attic after his accountant gave him the dreadful news. He must have been too distraught to even *look* at them any more.'

'Oh Mother, said Odelia, 'I'm sorry. I didn't mean

to upset you.' *This is all your fault*, she thought, glaring at the unfortunate knickerbockers. *If it wasn't for you, Father wouldn't have lost all his money and gone riding off into the evening to clear his head. And then he wouldn't have … wouldn't be …* She shook her head, as if she could shake away the sad ending that came next.

'It's fine,' said Mrs Hardluck-Smythe, smiling bravely. 'I'm glad they've found such *adventurous* new owners. They suit you, Captain. And you, Cook.'

'Course they suits me,' said Captain Blunderfuss. 'And you know what *else* would suit me even better?'

'Clean underwear?' guessed Mrs Hardluck-Smythe. 'A beard without bits of food stuck in it?'

'Marzipan fruits,' said the pirate. 'How about it? How about you write me some marzipan fruits and I'll promise not to wipe my nose on the curtains while no one's looking.'

'And I promise not to put my boots on your pillow next time,' added Cook.

Mrs Hardluck-Smythe shook her head. 'I'm not sure it works like that,' she said. 'I don't think I can conjure them out of thin air simply by adding them to the story.' She paused for a moment. 'By the way, what do you mean you promise not to put your boots on my pillow?' she added.

'I mean I'll put them on the other pillow next time,' said Cook. 'I'm not fussy—'

'It might not work for marzipan fruits but maybe you *could* add some extra clues to the treasure map,' interrupted Odelia, struck by a sudden burst of inspiration. 'The one from your book with the Ponsonby River and Batworth Woods. You wouldn't have to change much – just enough to show *exactly* where the X marking the spot is. And then once we've found the treasure, we'll be able to buy all the marzipan fruits we want.'

'I'm not sure it *needs* any more clues,' said her mother, growing defensive. 'I made it perfectly clear. Any pirate worth his salt should be able to find the treasure easily with the information provided.'

'And any writer worth her salt and pepper should be able to summon up a few lousy marzipan fruits for a pirate with the finest velvet leg coverings in the land,' replied Captain Blunderfuss.

'And some proper food for the kitchen,' added Cook. 'Something more than stale toasting bread. And a nice hammock to hang above the stove ...'

'How about it, lady?' demanded the captain. 'Are you going to get us our marzipan fruits and hammock or do we have to fight you for them?'

'Dada piwate fight fight!'

Uh-oh, thought Odelia. What was it Captain Blunderfuss had said earlier? *Treasure-hunting always ends with fighting.* Perhaps the same was true when it came to marzipan fruit negotiations. Just when things had been going so well ... 'Nobody's fighting *anybody,*' she said firmly, taking charge of the situation. 'Father's treasure is hidden somewhere in this house, and we need to find it before anyone else does. Mother, you take Sammy and check the nursery and bedrooms. Cook can start in the kitchen. Captain, you can do the drawing room and the dining room – but no more curtain-chopping this time – and I'll do everywhere else.'

'Oh Oddy,' said Mrs Hardluck-Smythe. 'We've already been through this. There *is* no treasure.'

'There is,' replied Odelia firmly. 'Father told me so himself,' she added, which was *almost* true. She still wasn't ready to admit she'd read his private journal. 'Please,' she begged. 'This is important.' *We have to find it before the Mayfair Mob come looking for it.*

'Very well,' agreed Mrs Hardluck-Smythe, scooping up Sammy and heading for the stairs. 'I need to jot down a few notes for my book anyway. What was it again? Ah yes, *putrid old pigeon-bum* ... perfect.'

Odelia started her own search in the bathroom, checking behind the basin pedestal and crawling under the clawfoot bath to look for hidden gold. She clambered up onto the windowsill and reached into the toilet cistern to check for lurking diamonds, but she was out of luck there too. Her windowsill perch *did* offer an excellent view of the back garden though, or what was left of it. The pirates must have dug up half the lawn, while everyone else was out at the museum, looking for their precious trousers.

Ding-dong. Odelia jumped as the doorbell chimed. *Oh no!* she thought, her heart fluttering with panic. *What if it's the Waterloo Woodworm Treatment Services?*

'I'll get it,' she cried, charging down the stairs before anyone could stop her. But if her hunch was right, she had no intention of opening the door and letting them in. She headed for the bay window in the front parlour instead, peering out from behind the curtains at the tall figure waiting on the doorstep, with darkening clouds clustered behind his head like a warning. A tall, elegant figure, with a long nose and a familiar-looking pair of green trousers, sticking out from beneath a large carrying case, with **WATERLOO WOODWORM TREATMENT SERVICES** stencilled on the front in big, black letters. Odelia gulped, ducking down out of sight as she tried to work out her next move. The net of criminal trickery and guile that had been closing in on them had just got a whole lot tighter.

CHAPTER 13

*I*t's time to call the police, decided the sensible,
law-abiding side of Odelia's brain.

*But what if they arrest Captain Blunderfuss for fish-
stealing?* pointed out the other side of her brain, equally
sensibly. *And what about Father's treasure? Why was
he keeping it such a secret in the first place? What if it's
stolen treasure?* Odelia hadn't even stopped to consider
that before. Surely her wax-moustached, steamed-
up-spectacled (and utterly respectable) father hadn't

been mixed up in anything untoward? But once she'd thought the thought, she couldn't unthink it. Was he some kind of pirate too? Maybe that explained why he was so keen on velvet knickerbockers.

She sank back down out of sight, listening to Captain Blunderfuss in the next room, singing as he searched:

'Old Davy Jones had a locker, had he,
Down at the bottom of the deep blue sea.
With rubies and diamonds and treasure to spare,
And jellyfish poo in his pirate hair.

Now Davy Jones had an old peg leg,
And his hairy bellybutton smelt of rotten egg.
He'd rubies and diamonds and treasure galore,
But his bum barnacles were terribly sore.'

The doorbell rang again.

'Oddy?' shouted Mrs Hardluck-Smythe. 'Who is it? What's going on?'

'Nothing to worry about, Mother,' Odelia shouted

back, hurrying out into the hall as the bell rang a third time. Criminals were so impatient! 'I had to er ... had to stop and retie my bootlaces, that's all. I'm just seeing who it is now though.'

She shrank back against the wall as the letterbox flap creaked open. As a pair of dark glittering eyes peered through the hole. 'Cooeee!' called a deep, well-spoken voice. 'It's Mr Bugwell from Waterloo Woodworm Treatment Services – I left a card for you earlier, regarding the threat to the structural integrity of your house due to a virulent strain of woodworm currently operating in the area.' The voice paused for a moment. 'A *very* virulent strain. Which is why I'm here to carry out a free, no-obligation examination of your property for you.'

If Odelia didn't know better, she might have been tempted to let him in. He sounded surprisingly posh and convincing for a wanted criminal. But she remembered what the policeman had told her earlier: *Looks a proper gentleman, he does, and sounds like one too. But don't let that fool you. He's a varmint all right, and no mistake.*

'You don't fool me,' she whispered, clenching her hands into fists. But maybe, just maybe, she could fool him …

She crept towards the door, keeping her back pressed against the wall to avoid being seen, and put on her deepest, gruffest, growliest voice. 'I don't know nothing about no woodworm examination,' she called back. 'I only just moved in. The old owners must've taken your card when they took everything else with them.'

The dark eyes blinked.

'And I mean, *everything.* Totally stripped the place, they did. Not so much as a single crumb of toast left when I got here today with my mean guard dog, Boxer.' Odelia let out a low doggy growl. A fierce, sharp-toothed bull terrier sort of growl.

Grrrr. Rufff! Rufff!

'Down boy, down,' she called.

Grrrrr.

'Sorry about that, Mr Bugwell. Boxer don't much like visitors, I'm afraid. He's *always* attacking them, he is. Takes after me, I guess. I'm a big, ferocious boxer myself, you see. I've knocked out more men than you've had hot dinners. Pummelled them to a pulp.'

The dark eyes narrowed. 'I see,' said so-called Mr Bugwell. 'And this all happened this afternoon, you say? I'm surprised I didn't see anything when I was here before. It's a big job, packing up an entire house ready to move.'

'They was in a hurry to go, I think. Said something about heading off to er … to France, to spend their family treasure. Pity they didn't leave any here for me. Still, never mind. At least there's no sign of any woodworm. Had a good check myself when I first arrived. So you've had a wasted journey I'm afraid.'

'I see,' repeated the voice. 'Who'd have thought it? Well in that case I'll wish you a good evening, Mr …?'

Odelia's mind went blank. 'Er … it's er …' She stared round the hall, looking for inspiration. *Mr Door? Mr Letterbox? Mr Mould-patch?*

'Mama!' came a loud Sammy-gurgle from upstairs.

'Brother,' Odelia finished. 'Mr Brother. Yes, that's

me. Mr Brother the champion boxer. Well, goodbye then.'

The voice said nothing. The letterbox snapped shut, and Odelia breathed out a huge sigh of relief. She'd done it! She'd thrown the thieves off the scent and saved the family fortune without getting anyone arrested. Or had she?

Snap.

The letter flap flew open again, and the dark eyes came peering through. 'One more thing, Mr Brother,' called the voice. 'Perhaps you could ask that dog of yours to keep the sea shanties down a bit. Anyone would think you were keeping a pirate in there too.'

Frogspawn and spider spit! cursed Odelia. He must have been out there for ages, listening in. Spying on them all. 'No. That'll be the big, scary policeman who lives next door,' she called back, so pleased with her quick thinking that she'd forgotten to disguise her voice. 'He's always singing shanties when he's watching out the window for signs of suspicious activity.' She'd also forgotten, momentarily, that 'Mr Brother' had only just moved in. He probably wouldn't even have *met* the neighbours yet. She could have cursed out loud when she realised her mistake. As it was, she had to settle for another silent curse instead. *Tadpoles and toe fluff! How can I have been so stupid?*

Odelia cleared her throat noisily and lowered her voice another octave or two. 'Er … sorry, I must have swallowed a fly there. Made me go all squeaky. What I meant to say was, I understand from the previous owners that my next-door neighbour is a highly trained police officer with a fondness for sea songs. I expect it was *him* you heard. Unless it was my *other* new neighbour who's some kind of famous detective specialising in unmasking criminal gangs … maybe *he* likes singing too. I wouldn't know, obviously, seeing as I've only just moved in.'

The dark eyes blinked twice. 'Yes. So you said,' observed the voice. 'In that case I'd better leave you to your unpacking. For now.' And with that the letterbox snapped shut again, followed by the sound of smart-heeled boots retreating down the front steps. Odelia raced to the front parlour and peered through the window to make sure he'd really gone this time. She watched his tall silhouette grow smaller and smaller as he headed down the road into the gathering clouds. But she couldn't shake the gnawing sense of unease in her tummy as she headed back upstairs to carry on her search. Just because he'd gone, didn't mean he wouldn't be coming back.

Despite Odelia's worries about 'Mr Bugwell' and the still-missing treasure (their combined searches having turned up nothing), the evening was surprisingly pleasant. Captain Blunderfuss entertained Mrs Hardluck-Smythe with his finest collection of insults, while Cook burned the toast and Odelia and Sammy played with Dog. Some fried fillets of fish to go with the burnt toast would have been even nicer, especially as they'd all missed lunch, but there'd been no sign of the morning's catch when Cook searched Sammy's perambulator.

There was a nasty moment after dinner, when Odelia's mother threatened to abandon Captain Blunderfuss on a desert island if he didn't stop picking his teeth with the nib of her fountain pen, and the captain threatened to make her walk the plank if she didn't stop being such a whinging whine-bucket. But Sammy managed to distract them both, before things got any more heated, by pulling himself up on the coffee table, giggling with triumph as he snatched up a spare slice of after-dinner toast from a nearby plate.

'Ah, will you look at that,' said Captain Blunderfuss. He put down his fountain pen toothpick and clapped his hand against his thigh in applause. 'Who's a clever boy then?'

'Well done, darling,' joined in Mrs Hardluck-Smythe, surreptitiously retrieving her pen and wiping the nib on her skirts. 'You're going to be strong and clever like your daddy, aren't you?'

'Dada,' Sammy agreed. 'Dada piwate spwat spwat.'

'Strong and clever like his sister, you mean,' said

Odelia, not wanting to be left out. Girls could be just as strong as boys. Just as clever. Just as good at saving the family from wicked thieves pretending to be woodworm experts. She scooped Sammy up into the air (half-chewed toast slice and all), proving to everyone how strong she could be, spinning him round and round above her head until they both grew dizzy.

'Oddy! Oddy piwate! Again! Again!'

Yes, it was a good evening. It was nice to have something else to think about – if only for a few hours – than thieves and policemen and missing treasure. Odelia's resolve was still as strong as ever, but by the time Mrs Hardluck-Smythe and Sammy finally retired for the night (taking their pen and toast with them), she was too exhausted to search any more. It had been such a long day – one of the longest, most exciting days she could remember – that when tiredness *did* eventually catch up with her, it was as much as she could manage to make up beds for the pirates on the sofa and chaise longue, before crawling back upstairs to her own room.

'I *will* find you though,' Odelia promised the missing

treasure as she snuggled down into her pillow, pulling the rough covers up to her still-sooty chin. 'Just you wait and see. I'll find where you're hiding and make everything all right again.' Of course, the treasure, being missing treasure, said nothing. *Almost everything*, she corrected herself. All the treasure in the world still wouldn't bring Father back.

Sleep well, little Oddy Odd Sock, she imagined him saying, as her last coherent thoughts slipped away behind her eyelids. As she sank seamlessly into dreams of snuff-scented fingers ruffling through freshly brushed hair. Dreams of sailing down the Serpentine with Sammy on board a pirate ship plagued by woodworm.

She was still dreaming when the thieves came, under the noisy cover of rain, smashing their way in through the sash window in the dining room. Still dreaming as they searched the ground floor, turning over furniture and pulling up rugs. Tugging out shelves and emptying drawers into the middle of the floor. Odelia slept on, oblivious, as they made their way up to the first floor, towards the nursery, her mind still full of nonsense and wonder.

It was Sammy's cry that finally roused her.

'Dada? Dada?' The sound came creeping along the landing to find her, burrowing its way into her drowsy ears. 'Dada?'

Shhh, thought Odelia, turning over onto her other side. *Go back to sleep, Sammy, there's a good boy.*

But then the cry changed from playful to something else. 'Dada? Dada?' It sounded confused now. Worried. No, more than that. It sounded scared. 'DADA!' A loud piercing scream. 'NO, NO, NO!' And then nothing.

Odelia sat up in bed with a start, listening to the space where her brother's cries should have been. But all she could hear was rain.

Something was wrong.

Something was *very* wrong.

CHAPTER 14

Odelia tore along the moonlit landing in her nightgown, the bitter taste of panic rising in her throat. *Maybe it's a nightmare*, she told herself, skidding past the top of the stairs. *A bad dream, that's all.* But the tight knot in her stomach didn't believe her for one moment. Deep down she knew something bad had happened.

And there it was. The empty crib told Odelia everything she needed to know. That and the loud disagreement drifting up from the hallway.

'But we're not done yet,' said a gruff voice. 'We haven't found the treasure. You said–'

'Forget about the treasure,' cut in a second voice. A posh voice that sounded suspiciously like Mr Bugwell. 'There's no time. He'll have woken half the house by now. Let's just take the baby and go.'

A third voice joined the conversation as Odelia stood in the empty nursery, frozen with shock. 'Easy for you to say. How am I supposed to lug him *and* my loot bag all the way up bird quiche? Walk? I don't know why you nabbed him in the first place. What are we supposed to do with a baby, for crying out loud?'

Bird quiche? Even in Odelia's frozen state she knew that didn't sound right.

'Don't you worry your thieving head about that,' said Mr Bugwell. 'I've got a plan. There's more than one way to skin a cat, you know. Hand your loot bag to Rogers and concentrate on keeping the child quiet. Do you think you can manage that?'

'What? You never said nothing about skinning cats. Kidnapping – I mean *baby*-napping – is one thing, but

I draw the line at that.'

'It's just a saying, you dithering dunce. Hurry up now, let's go, before someone catches us.'

The sound of the front door closing behind them jolted Odelia out of her stupor. What was she doing, standing there like a lemon while they whisked her baby brother away? She had to stop them. She had to save Sammy.

'Come back with my little brother,' she called into the darkness as she tore down the stairs after them, 'or I'll set my pirates on you. They'll make you walk the plank and feed you to the sharks. See how you like that!' But it was too late. By the time she reached the front door, flinging it open and shouting after them into the wet gloom, the thieves had disappeared.

Odelia didn't know what to do first. Chase out into the rain after them or wake Mother? Fetch the police or fetch Captain Blunderfuss and Cook? But it seemed that fate and a rumbling pirate tummy had already decided for her.

'Dribbling duckspit! My belly's so empty I can

hardly hear myself snore. I wonder if the old witch has got me my marzipan fruits yet. I could eat the whole box right now. Make that three boxes ... Shiver me thimbles, what's going on out here?' called the captain, appearing in the darkened doorway.

'It's S-Sammy,' Odelia told him, wiping at the sudden tears coursing down her cheeks. 'They've taken Sammy.'

'Who has? Admiral Arbuckle? I always knew he was a trumped-up trouser toff. I didn't realise he was a baby-snatcher too.'

'No,' said Odelia. 'Well, yes, sort of.' The lines between fact and fiction were so blurred by now, she couldn't be sure of anything. *Was* it Admiral Arbuckle she'd spotted in the park that morning? Had he escaped from Mother's book and disguised himself as Mr Bugwell to try and worm his way into their house? Or had her mother used one of the newspaper articles about the Mayfair Mob as inspiration for his character? Which came first? Not that it mattered. *Nothing* mattered any more apart from getting her baby brother back. 'He and his gang were looking for Father's treasure,' she explained between sobs, 'but they've taken Sammy instead.'

'What? They've taken the nipper? The little smiley feller with the toast and the smelly bottom?' For a moment Captain Blunderfuss looked like *he* might cry too, but instead he took a deep snortling sniff, and cursed for all he was worth. 'Ringworm and rotten eggs! That slimy-toaded, baboon-bottom-breath piece of bellybutton snot! I'll box his wax-infested ears.' He shook his hook. 'I'll flibber his gibbet and pickle his spleen. Don't you worry, Sub-ordinary,' he added, patting her gently on the shoulder. 'We'll get the little feller back somehow. By hook or by crook. Or by Cook,' he added as an afterthought. 'Wake up, you dozy dogfish, we've got a baby to save.'

Odelia nodded, wiping her nose on the back of her hand. 'I suppose I should let Mother know what's happened …' The very thought filled her with horror though. She remembered how Mrs Hardluck-Smythe had crumpled to the floor when the police officer told her about Father, her legs melting beneath her like jelly. She remembered the unladylike howl of pain her mother had let out – an endless, anguished cry, like a wild animal caught in a trap. She remembered her mother's unkempt hair and the dark shadows under her reddened eyes in those first terrible days. It was Sammy who'd given her a reason to keep living. Sammy who'd pulled her through. Pulled them *both* through. He'd been the only ray of light in Odelia's life since Father died too.

'No time for that,' said Captain Blunderfuss, as Cook emerged, rubbing his eyes and yawning. 'The longer we stand here snivelling, the longer it'll take to find 'em. Did you see which way they went?'

Odelia shook her head. 'They were already gone by the time I got downstairs. But I heard one of them say something about walking … and bird quiche, and how he was going to manage with the baby.' The thought of some big, brutish thief manhandling Sammy like a stolen bag of loot was almost too much to bear, but she gulped back the rest of her tears and forced the image away again. Sammy needed her to be strong for him. Strong and focused.

'I made a seagull quiche once,' piped up Cook. 'I tried to, anyway, only the seagull flew away again before I'd finished adding the egg mixture.'

'Wait, maybe it wasn't bird *quiche*,' said Odelia, refusing to be distracted with tales of unbaked seagulls. 'Maybe it was bird *cage*. Yes, Birdcage Walk. One of the roads that runs down from Buckingham Palace. That must be where he meant.'

'Then let's go,' said the pirate. 'Don't you worry, little feller,' he called, as they hurried out into the night, with Dog padding along behind them. 'We'll have you back safe and sound before you knows it.'

The rain had stopped again, thankfully. Odelia was chilly enough as it was in her nightgown and bare feet – if only she'd thought to put her boots on before rushing out! – and the shock of it all had left her cold on the inside too. Her teeth were chattering like Spanish castanets before they'd even reached the end of Hadlington Gardens.

'Here,' said Captain Blunderfuss, taking off his tattered pirate coat and draping it across her shoulders. He shot her a gruff smile. 'We can't have you freezing to death now, can we?'

It was ten sizes too big and smelt of stale sweat and rotten fish, but Odelia slipped her hands down inside the coat sleeves and smiled back at him. The closest she could manage to a smile, anyway, with Sammy still missing and a pit of worry opening up inside her. 'Thank you,' she said. 'You're the best pirate captain I've ever met, you know.'

'And you're the best sub-ordinary *I've* ever met,' said Captain Blunderfuss. 'I've been thinking of giving you a promotion, in fact. How does second-in-commode sound?'

'Do you mean second-in-*command*?' asked Odelia.

'What about me?' Cook frowned. 'I thought I was your second-in-commode.'

'Or maybe you could be my new ship's basin?' Captain Blunderfuss nodded to himself. 'Yes, that sounds even better. What do you say?' He held out his hook for her to shake.

Odelia assumed he meant 'bosun' rather than 'basin'. Not that she knew what a bosun was, exactly – something to do with anchors and sails, maybe? – but she *did* know what a basin was. Unlike Captain Blunderfuss and Cook, judging by the looks of them (not to mention the smell). But she took the captain's cold metal hook in her fingers and shook on it all the same. 'I'd be honoured.' Hopefully basins were better at saving baby brothers than sub-ordinaries. 'Aye aye and raise the mainsail,' she added, battling against the growing pit of worry inside. It seemed to be getting bigger with every step. 'Ship's Basin reporting for duty, Captain ... Wait! What's that?' She pointed to a soggy-looking ball of something floating in a puddle by her bare feet.

'What's what?' asked the captain. He picked up the soggy ball and examined it in the glow of a nearby streetlamp. 'Mmm, looks like bread to me ... smells like it too. Tastes like pavement with a hint of dribble. Perhaps a bird dropped it? I heard there's vultures nesting round here.'

Odelia didn't need to lick it to know what it was. 'No. It's not bread,' she said. 'It's toast.'

'There's a big difference,' agreed Cook. But Odelia wasn't finished yet.

'And it wasn't vultures that dropped it,' she said, her eyes shining. 'It was Sammy! He was still clutching his half-sucked piece of toast when he went to bed last night, remember? The one he found on the coffee table. Which means we must be on the right track.'

'Well don't just stand there chitter-chatting then,' said Captain Blunderfuss. 'Let's go!'

'Next stop Bird Quiche Walk,' added Cook with a wink. 'We'll find him, you'll see,' he said kindly. 'He'll be tucked up back in bed before you know it. And so will we, with any luck.'

Odelia tossed the toast down to Dog and hurried after the captain. 'We're coming, Sammy,' she called into the night. 'We'll save you,' she promised.

CHAPTER 15

The city looked and sounded very different at three o'clock in the morning. The elegant thoroughfares of Mayfair were almost deserted, the light from the streetlamps lending them an eerie, ghostly air. The roads were oddly quiet too. There were no horses or wheels clattering over the cobbles. No shouts. No cries. Only the occasional miaow from Dog and the *clack* of the pirates' boots echoing behind Odelia as she led them down towards Green Park, keeping a sharp lookout for any more signs of dropped toast.

There was no toast to be seen in the park though, just homeless people sleeping huddled together for warmth. *Once we find Father's treasure I'll come back and share some with you,* Odelia promised them silently as she hurried past. *But I need to save Sammy first.*

On she raced past a ghostly-looking Buckingham Palace, its enormous white gateposts topped by flickering gas lamps. Although it was still the Queen's official London residence, Victoria preferred to live elsewhere after the death of her beloved Albert all those years before. Odelia always imagined the big, fancy rooms inside Buckingham Palace lying empty and abandoned like the famous 'ghost ship' *The Mary Celeste*, but in truth there were probably hundreds of servants scurrying around inside, keeping the place running in the Queen's absence.

'This is it,' she announced, as they turned onto Birdcage Walk. 'This is the road the thieves were talking about.' But there was no sign of any thieves now. No sign of Sammy. Odelia refused to give up hope though, chasing down the street in search of her brother. In search of another ball of soggy toast, to prove she was on the right track.

'There!' said Cook, pointing to something round and pale in the middle of the road. 'What's that?'

Odelia pounced on it before Dog could, a burst of fresh hope flaring in her chest. But it wasn't soggy toast, it was a hard pebble. *Blast and badger-spit!* And the 'ball of toast' on the corner of Horse Guards Road turned out to be an unusually round splat of bird poo. *Slug-slime and … and …* It was no good. Odelia was too disappointed to even finish her curse.

'Which way now?' asked Cook.

'I don't know,' admitted Odelia, trying not to cry. On towards Big Ben and the Houses of Parliament, or down to Westminster Abbey? Along Whitehall, or back around the outside of St James's Park? There was no way of guessing. The trail had gone as cold as her poor frozen feet.

The last flickers of hope spluttered and died as the heavens opened again, sending sharp needles of rain cascading down on Odelia's head. She pulled the captain's coat tighter across her chest, hunching down inside the oversized collar in a futile attempt to stay dry. A nearby tree offered a brief moment of shelter, but the rain soon found its way through the leaves, hammering down on her head and streaming off the end of her nose.

'Flibbering fishtails,' gasped Captain Blunderfuss, 'I'm wetter than an octopus's armpit. How are we supposed to find the little feller in this?'

'We can't,' said Odelia, fresh tears mingling with the rivers already coursing down her cheeks. The impossibility of the task weighed heavier on her shoulders than the captain's sodden coat. 'He's gone … Oh Sammy,' she wailed into the rain. 'I'm sorry. It's all my fault. *I'm* the one who told the thieves where the treasure was. *I'm* the one who got you stolen. I knew Mr Bugwell wasn't really a woodworm specialist, and I still let my guard down. I still let him and his mob carry you off in the middle of the night.'

'Hey, that's enough of that.' The captain pulled

her into a wet, smelly hug, his dripping beard tickling at the top of her head. 'No more blaming yourself. Got it? And no more tears. The last thing I need is a leaky basin.'

'Aye aye, Captain,' sniffed Odelia, squeezing herself even tighter into the hug. If she shut her eyes and blocked out the rain and the cold and the smell, she could almost imagine it was Father wrapping his arms round her. *Almost*.

'Now then, let's get you home before you catch euphonium. I can feel your timbers shivering from here.'

Pneumonia, you mean. Odelia shook her head, her cheek scratching against the pirate's shirt button. 'I can't,' she whispered. 'I can't leave him.'

Dog wound himself round her ankles, crying pitifully.

'Nonsense,' said Captain Blunderfuss. 'You'll be no good to anyone if you stay out here. Not me and not the little feller, either. How's he going to feel when he gets back home to find you dead and buried from too much cold and rain?'

'But … but …'

'Buttons and bum cheeks,' said the pirate, dismissively. 'And what about that meddling mother of yours? She might be a wormy old witch who deserves to be fed to the sharks for saddling me with a hook and a broomstick, but you and the little chap seem to like her. What's *she* going to think when she wakes up and finds you gone as well?'

'He's right, you know,' agreed Cook, scooping up the bedraggled-looking Dog.

Odelia imagined her mother rising early, as always. Imagined her creeping into the nursery to begin work, and discovering the cold, empty cot. She imagined her cry of surprise. Imagined her hurrying back along the landing to Odelia's own room to find another empty bed. Another cry – more fearful this time. She imagined her searching the house ... checking the empty perambulator ... tearing up and down the street in panic ... banging on the neighbours' doors ... *Poor Mother. As if losing Father isn't enough.*

'All right,' said Odelia, admitting defeat. 'I'll go home. I'll get myself dry and I'll tell Mother what's happened. She deserves that much. But I'm not giving up. I have to find Sammy. I *have* to save him.'

'No, Basin,' said Captain Blunderfuss, giving her another wet squeeze. '*We* have to find him. We're a team now: you, me and Cook. We'll save him together, we will.'

They were too late. Mrs Hardluck-Smythe was already waiting there in the hallway, red-eyed and ashen-faced, when they arrived back, dripping on the doormat. She was clutching a letter of some kind in her hand, but she dropped it at the sight of Odelia, flinging her arms round her daughter and clinging on for dear life.

'Oh Oddy, thank goodness,' she cried. 'I thought they'd taken you too.'

'I'm s-s-sorry,' stammered Odelia, shivering in her wet nightie despite the warmth of her mother's arms. *I'm sorry for running off without telling you. I'm sorry for losing Sammy. I'm sorry for everything.*

'Oh Oddy.' Mrs Hardluck-Smythe released her from the hug in order to pick up the fallen letter. 'Someone's taken Sammy,' she said, as if Odelia didn't already know. As if she and the pirates had been racing through the dark and rain for fun. 'And now they're demanding a ransom for his safe return.'

'A ram's bum?' Captain Blunderfuss's sodden tricorn hat had slipped down over his ears under the weight of so much water. He squeezed out the front of his shirt to make a little puddle on the floor. 'Where are we supposed to get one of those from? Why didn't they ask for something better? Like velvet trousers? Or marzipan fruits?'

'A *ransom*,' said Odelia, pushing his hat back up so he could hear properly. 'It means …' She paused, realising she didn't actually know *what* it meant. There was still a long way to go before she reached the 'R' section of Father's dictionary. If the thieves had asked for a *vintage Valencian vaporiser* or a *voluminous valise*, she'd have had no trouble explaining.

'It means I have to pay them money if I want to

see my baby boy again,' said Mrs Hardluck-Smythe, dissolving into fresh tears at the very thought. 'M-money I d-don't have. Oh Sammy!'

Odelia prised the note from her mother's fingers, hoping to spot something that could help them. A clue as to where they were keeping Sammy. But there was no address. No date. No *Dear Mrs Hardluck-Smythe*. Just an ugly string of words cut out of the newspaper, demanding money for his return:

If **YOU** Want to *See* **YOUR** Baby AGAIN bring **£500 TO** the band**STAND** in **Hyde Park** at SIX **p**.m. TODAY. **WARNING**, Do **NOT** tell the **POLICE** or **ELSE**.

'They're giving me one day to raise five hundred pounds,' said Mrs Hardluck-Smythe, wringing her hands in despair. 'Where am I going to find that sort of money in one measly day?'

Captain Blunderfuss peered over Odelia's shoulder at the note. 'What about the treasure? Maybe they'd swap the little feller for *that* instead?'

'Treasure?' repeated Mrs Hardluck-Smythe, with a

strange, sobbing sort of laugh. 'There *is* no treasure. We searched the house from top to bottom yesterday, and we didn't find anything.'

'It must be here somewhere,' insisted Odelia. 'It *has* to be. That's what the woodworm thieves – the Mayfair Mob, I mean – were after too. They were looking for Father's treasure, just like us, only they couldn't find it, so they took ...' She sniffed. 'They took Sammy instead.'

Mrs Hardluck-Smythe shook her head. 'I already told you, Oddy. Father barely had a penny to his name when he died. No gold or priceless jewels. No rubies. No diamonds. Just trousers.' Her eyes narrowed. 'I curse the day he ever *heard* of Mr Hose and his velvet knickerbockers.'

'But he *did*,' insisted Odelia. '*The greatest treasure in the world right here under my own roof.* That's what he said.' It didn't matter any more if Mother thought she'd been snooping. There were more important things at stake now. '*A treasure above all others, to be guarded with my very life.* I read it in his diary.'

'No, my darling, no,' said her mother. 'You must have got confused ...'

'I'll show you.' Odelia handed back the ransom note and started off towards the stairs.

'Oh no you don't,' Captain Blunderfuss called after her. 'Not until you've put some dry clothes on. You're shaking harder than a jellyfish with fleas.'

'But, but ...'

'Butterscotch and bunions,' said the pirate, batting away her objections. 'We don't want no wet basins round here. Clothes first – and that's an order. And you can bring me and Cook down some fresh trousers, too, from the crow's nest. That's another order. You're not the only one whose timbers are shivering.'

Odelia bit back her frustration. She knew he was right – she'd be no good to anyone, least of all Sammy, if she caught pneumonia – but the need to find Father's treasure was more urgent than ever now. She could almost feel the wasted minutes slipping through their fingers. 'Aye aye, Captain,' she answered, handing him back his coat and stumbling up the stairs in her hurry to return to the search.

She threw on her pirate bloomers, shirt and black ribbon belt from the day before and wrapped a blanket across her shoulders for extra warmth. There – that was better. Her limbs still felt like ice but at least she *could* actually feel them now. Then she dashed up to the attic and grabbed two fresh pairs of knickerbockers from the trunk the pirates had unearthed – matching mauve ones this time – before hurrying back down to fetch her father's diary, praying that the thieves hadn't already taken it.

Judging by the looks of things, they hadn't got as far as Mother's bedroom though. *Thank goodness.* Everything seemed to be in its proper place. No upturned furniture. No drawers pulled out across the floor. No sign of any disturbance. And there was Father's Golden Jubilee biscuit tin waiting under the bed, right where Odelia had left it. She dug through the bow ties and cravats and snatched up the precious diary.

'We'll find the treasure this time, Father,' she whispered into the quiet of the room. 'Wherever you've hidden it, we'll find it. We're going to save Sammy, I promise.' She scooped up a couple of Mother's shawls on her way out, for Captain Blunderfuss and Cook, then tore back downstairs to show them Mr Hardluck-Smythe's last precious words.

'Here it is,' said Odelia, turning to the end of Father's diary. She and Mrs Hardluck-Smythe had moved into the dining room to give the pirates some trouser-changing privacy. 'This is the bit I was telling you about. *I must be grateful for what I <u>do</u> have,*' she read, '*instead of lamenting what is already gone. How can all be lost when I still have the greatest treasure in the world right here under my own roof? A treasure above all others, to be guarded with my very life. Yes, that is what I must focus on now. Perhaps a ride along the Thames will help clear my head and shift this wretched cold …*'

Mrs Hardluck-Smythe let out a choked sob. 'Oh Percy,' she murmured, clutching a hand to her heart.

'Why didn't you stay home and let me take care of you? A hot toddy and an early night were what you needed, not a bicycle ride. How could you have left us like this? Abandoned us to debt and hunger? To baby-stealing thieves and criminals?'

Odelia took hold of her mother's other hand, squeezing her fingers tight. 'It wasn't Father's fault,' she said. 'It wasn't *anyone's* fault.'

'If anything happens to Sammy ... if they hurt so much as a single downy hair on his precious head, I'll ... I'll ...'

'No one's going to hurt him,' said Odelia. 'We're going to find Father's treasure and get him back safe and sound. You'll see,' she said, sounding more confident than she felt. 'Everything's going to be all right.'

'But your father didn't *have* any treasure,' insisted Mrs Hardluck-Smythe through her tears. 'None of this makes any sense. What else does he say?'

'That's it,' said Odelia. 'That's all he wrote. At least, I *think* it is. That's as far as I got before Captain Blunderfuss came in with the Ponsonby-Smarms' carp.' She turned over the page, to make doubly sure, but there was nothing written on the other side. How could there be? That was Mr Hardluck-Smythe's final diary entry. His last ever words … Odelia's throat tightened, her eyes stinging as she stared at the empty page. 'Nothing else,' she whispered.

'No,' said her mother, peeling the diary out of her hand. 'Look there – the pages have got stuck together.' She crossed over to the hole in the curtains, holding the diary up to the first stirrings of daylight outside. 'Yes, I can see writing!'

Cartwheels and cuttlefish! 'What does it say?' cried Odelia, despair turning back to hope. 'Is it about the treasure? Is it a clue?'

CHAPTER 16

Mrs Hardluck-Smythe teased the top corners apart with her fingernails, easing one page away from the other with exasperating slowness.

Odelia wriggled and fidgeted, willing her to hurry up. *Come on, come on, tell me what it says.*

'There,' announced her mother in triumph, smoothing out the freshly separated pages. 'Let's see now …'

Moth balls and marigolds. The wait was unbearable.

What was taking her so long?

'Oh!' cried Mrs Hardluck-Smythe.

Odelia couldn't decide if it was a good 'oh' or a bad 'oh'. 'Oh' as in 'Oh, what a surprise, the treasure was in my sewing basket all along?' or 'Oh' as in 'Oh no, it was hidden in that stuffed deer head we sold six months ago'? 'What is it?' she asked.

'Oh Oddy.'

'*Please*,' Odelia begged. 'Just tell me what it says.'

Her mother nodded. 'I'm sorry, darling. I was right – there never was any treasure. At least not the kind you're thinking of … *And then home to my beloved family*,' she read, wiping away a tear, '*to my beautiful, constant Constance and my little Oddy Odd Sock, the most precious treasure any man could ask for – glittering jewels to brighten the darkest of dark days. Even in the midst of such misfortune, I'm still the luckiest man alive.*'

'What was that? Glittering jewels, did you say? Where are they, then?' called Captain Blunderfuss from the doorway, waving his sodden treasure map and looking very un-pirate-like indeed in his new knickerbockers and borrowed shawl. The pattern of pink roses across his chest would have had Odelia laughing out loud if her heart wasn't so busy breaking.

'My little Oddy Odd Sock,' she murmured. 'That's what he called me when he came to say goodnight.' *It was me*, she thought, filling up with a mixture of love and despair. Deep, aching love … and even deeper despair. *I was the treasure all along. Me and mother … and Sammy.* She could almost hear her father's voice speaking the words as he wrote them. His last words. Could almost feel his arms reaching out to her again across the chasm of those long, empty months without him. Almost. But he wasn't the luckiest man alive, was he? Luck had deserted him just as it deserted them all, snatching him away forever. *And now Sammy's gone too, and there is no treasure and now … and now …*

'No, Captain,' said Mrs Hardluck-Smythe softly, fresh tears streaming down her cheeks. 'There aren't any jewels. There never were. *We* were my husband's treasure. His family. Which means we're right back where we started. With nothing to offer the thieves and no hope of saving Sammy.'

'Dogs' breath and dandelions,' cursed the pirate, the treasure map slipping, useless, from his fingers. It was a kind sort of curse though. The sort of curse that was followed by a revolting handkerchief, rescued from a pair of wet knickerbockers and held out like an offering. Mrs Hardluck-Smythe took one look at the stained, still-dripping rag and shuddered, hurriedly wiping her eyes with the side of her finger instead. But Captain Blunderfuss wasn't finished yet. 'There's *always* hope,' he told her, blowing his nose on the unwanted handkerchief. 'We'll fight every last one of those miserable maggots if we have to. We'll flibber their gibbets and scuttle their butts.'

'We'll beat 'em like eggs,' added Cook, appearing in the doorway behind him, sporting a fetching lavender shawl with a tasselled fringe. 'We'll whip 'em like cream and mash 'em like spuds.'

'They're right,' Odelia told her mother, shaking herself out of her grief. Out of despair. There was no time for that now. 'Not about the fighting – although

I'll take on every thief in London if it helps get Sammy back – but about not giving up. As long as we've still got hope, we've still got a chance. There has to be *something* we can do. We could ask the neighbours …' The suggestion died away to nothing on her lips. As if Mrs Ponsonby-Smarm would hand over five hundred pounds to help *anybody*.

'Perhaps we *should* go to the police,' said Mrs Hardluck-Smythe. 'It's got to be better than fighting. We wouldn't stand a chance against a dangerous criminal gang.'

Odelia shook her head. 'No. You saw what their note said: *Do not tell the police or else.*' She didn't know what that meant, exactly, but the thought of anyone carrying out an 'or else' on her little brother made her feel sick and shivery inside. 'There's got to be another way.' She glanced round the room for inspiration, as if the answer might be right there waiting for them … but maybe it was!

'The treasure map,' she cried, pointing to the bedraggled roll of paper at the pirate's feet. 'That's it!'

Captain Blunderfuss rested his hook on her shoulder. 'You heard what she said, Basin. There *is* no treasure – map or no map. There never was.'

'I know that,' said Odelia. 'But the map wasn't *always* in your pocket, was it? It wasn't there when you first arrived. When you were hiding behind the curtains pretending to be Father.'

'I wasn't pretending to be no one. I don't even know how I got here. One minute I was on board *The Sea Lion's Bellybutton*, thinking about marzipan and watching the sun set, and the next thing I knew it was morning and I was here, *still* thinking about marzipan and you were …'

'Yes, yes, we know all that,' Odelia said, although that wasn't strictly true. The sudden appearance of the pirate in the nursery was as much of a mystery as ever. But they knew the *rest* of the story well enough, and there was no time to spare on reminiscence. Every passing minute, every single wasted second, brought the thieves' six o'clock deadline closer. 'But did you have the treasure map then? That's the bit we need to know.'

'No,' piped up Mrs Hardluck-Smythe, answering for him. 'He can't have done because I hadn't written it yet. That was afterwards.'

'Exactly!' Fresh hope flared in Odelia's chest. 'You wrote it into your story and it magically appeared in his pocket. So why can't you do the same thing with the money? Write something about the captain discovering five hundred pounds stuffed inside a borrowed shawl … no wait, inside a biscuit tin,' she said, thinking of her father's commemorative Golden Jubilee one upstairs. 'And then we can use *that* to pay the ransom.'

Mrs Hardluck-Smythe didn't look convinced. 'As I said yesterday, I'm not sure it works like that. I added in a new scene before I went to bed last night, with Captain Blunderfuss and Cook getting attacked by a flock of angry albatrosses – sorry about that, I'll make sure you both escape – and there's been no sign of any albatrosses round here.'

'What about vultures?' said the pirate. 'Do they count?'

'Please,' Odelia begged. 'Just try it. For Sammy. I'll

go and get the biscuit tin so you can imagine it properly and then meet you in the nursery.'

Mrs Hardluck-Smythe refilled the ink in her fountain pen and got to work. *Cook grabbed hold of Dog and dived into an empty rum barrel to escape, while Captain Blunderfuss shook his hook at the squawking birds.* 'There you go, Cook, I told you I'd keep you safe,' said Mrs Hardluck-Smythe.

'Thank you,' said Cook. 'Would it be all right if I had a little sleep while I was there? All this rushing around in the middle of the night is starting to catch up with me,' he added with a yawn.

'*Cook was soon fast asleep, curled up tight in his cosy barrel, but there were no spare barrels for the captain to hide in,*' Mrs Hardluck-Smythe murmured to herself as she wrote.

' *"Leave me alone, you putrid pigeon-bums," he roared up at the vicious birds, shaking inside with fear.*'

'What do you mean, *shaking inside with fear?*' demanded the captain. 'I'm not scared of nothing or nobody. Apart from squids. And you'd be scared of them, too, if you'd had poisonous ink squirted in your eye.'

'Shhh,' said Odelia. 'Don't distract her. She needs to concentrate.'

Mrs Hardluck-Smythe paused for a moment at the end of the sentence. 'Hmmm let's see … I know! *"My catapult!" roared the pirate, ducking for cover as another squawking flurry of wings and beaks bore down on him from above …*'

'A catapult? What kind of namby-pamby pirate do you take me for?'

'Wait,' said Mrs Hardluck-Smythe. '*Do* albatrosses squawk?'

'It doesn't matter,' said Odelia, 'keep writing. Get to the bit with the money.'

' *"If I can just reach it in time…" he whimpered, hobbling along the deck as fast as his peg leg could carry him …*'

The captain snorted. 'Pigswill and poppycock! I've never whimpered in my life!'

'... *diving headfirst down into the hold as the birds lunged for him again, smacking his elbow on the ladder as he fell.*'

'I didn't even whimper when I lost my leg to that shark. *He* was the one whimpering by the time *I'd* finished with him.'

'*But clumsy Captain Blunderfuss ignored the shooting pains running up his arm ...*'

The pirate snorted. '*Brave* Captain Blunderfuss, you mean. *Heroic* Captain Blunderfuss. *Handsome* Captain Blunderfuss.'

Mrs Hardluck-Smythe took no notice. '*... ignored the shooting pains running up his arm and began searching the hold for his trusty catapult.*'

'My cutlass, you mean ... Or my pistol. No, wait, a cannon. Why can't I have a cannon? BOOM! Take that, you filthy feather-buckets!'

'*"But what's this?" he cried, picking up a commemorative Golden Jubilee biscuit tin. A cream and red tin, with a picture of Queen Victoria on the lid and the royal crest in the top corner.'*

'And a dent in one of the sides,' added Odelia. 'Don't forget the dent.'

' *"A biscuit tin?" cried Captain Blunderfuss. "With a dent in one of the sides? Wherever did that come from?" He frowned to himself. "Why, that meddlin' mongoose-chops Admiral Arbuckle must have dropped it when he was robbing me of my latest loot." He forgot all about the albatrosses waiting to attack him on the deck. He forgot all about steering the ship. He was too busy thinking about biscuits ...'*

'How about if I left the steering to my sub-ordinary instead?' suggested the captain. 'My basin, I mean.'

'Really? I get to steer the ship?' asked Odelia, picturing herself at the helm, doing battle with wild winds and enormous crashing waves … and albatrosses. But then she remembered about Sammy – how could she have forgotten? – and pushed the image away again, with a guilty start.

Mrs Hardluck-Smythe took no notice. After the

briefest of pen-sucking pauses, she was off again. ' *"I wonder if there are any left," he mused, giving the tin a shake. But the soft rattling noise didn't sound much like biscuits. At least, not hard, crunchy ones with sugar sprinkles on top. Maybe the sea air had made them soft and mushy? Luckily, Captain Blunderfuss was a pirate of simple tastes, and a soggy biscuit was better than no biscuit at all ...'*

'Oi, you prattle-mouthed pudding. Who are you calling simple?'

'He prised open the lid with his trusty hook and gasped out loud. It wasn't biscuits at all. It was money! "Snortling snail shells!" he cried. "There must be five hundred pounds in here!"'

'You should add a bit more while you're at it,' suggested Cook with a yawn. 'Then we can spend the rest on some *real* biscuits, once we get the little nipper back.'

'No. Five hundred pounds is fine,' said Mrs Hardluck-Smythe, laying her pen down on the desk. She looked paler than ever. 'Getting Sammy back is the only thing that matters now.'

Odelia gave the tin a hopeful shake, just like Captain Blunderfuss had in the story. 'Let's see if it's worked.' Her hands were trembling as she prised off the lid – slowly, slowly – hardly daring to look. *Please let it be full of money. Please, please, please.*

CHAPTER 17

Bow ties – *that's* what the tin was full of. Bow ties, cravats and more bow ties. Just like before. *Where is the money? Why hasn't it worked?* Odelia emptied the tin out over the floor, to make doubly sure. But there were no crisp notes hiding underneath. Nothing but neckwear.

'Oh,' sighed Mrs Hardluck-Smythe, looking more wistful than disappointed. 'I'd forgotten these were here.' She picked up a red silk cravat and pressed it to her lips. 'This was one of his favourites. Your father always looked handsome in red.'

'Perhaps it's too soon.' Odelia put the lid back on the empty tin, pressing it down extra tight. 'Maybe the writing magic needs more time to work.'

'And this is the one he was wearing when he asked for my hand in marriage ...' Mrs Hardluck-Smythe stared into the distance, her eyes glazed with happier memories. 'When he knelt down on one knee and ...' She shook her head, dragging herself back to the full awfulness of the present. 'We could sell some of these – that would be a start. Not much of a start, though. Not enough to help Sammy. Oh, Oddy, whatever shall we do?'

Captain Blunderfuss answered for her. 'Forget about the biscuit tin and write me a cannon instead. That'll teach the thieving thunderbugs to mess with *our* little feller. BOOM! Bye bye baby-snatchers. BOOM! Take that, you villainous varmints! BOOM! BOOM! BOOM!'

'No! That's a terrible idea,' Odelia told him. 'What

if we hit Sammy by mistake? We just need to wait for the magic to kick in.'

Mrs Hardluck-Smythe didn't look convinced. 'We can't sit around waiting for something that might never happen. We *have* to get that money from somewhere. I've already pawned all my jewellery. The only thing left of any value is my wedding ring.' She looked down at her hand and sighed. 'But your father would understand. Yes,' she said, 'I'll take it down to the pawnbroker's as soon as they open, and the bow ties, and then ... and then ...'

'What's a prawn broker?' interrupted Captain Blunderfuss.

'Sounds a bit fishy to me,' Cook said as he clambered into Sammy's empty crib, tucking his bony pirate knees under his stubbly chin and rearranging the lavender shawl like a blanket.

'No, a *pawn*broker,' Odelia explained. 'It's someone who lends you money in exchange for something valuable, like a necklace or a watch. There's one down the end of that cobbled lane we passed yesterday.

They're easy to spot because of the three gold balls they always have hanging outside. If you pay the pawnbroker back, with interest, you get your item returned to you, and if you don't, he sells it to someone else.'

'So if we had a sparkly diamond necklace, we could swap it for money?' said the captain. 'For Sammy?'

Odelia nodded. 'Only the closest thing *I've* got to a sparkly diamond is my lucky marble. And it's not turning out to be very lucky after all … Wait, where are you going?' Captain Blunderfuss had tightened his shawl round his shoulders with an air of determination and was heading for the nursery door.

'Just going for a quick wee,' he replied, looking decidedly shifty. 'In one of the flowerpots. Don't worry, I'll be back for breakfast.'

Odelia was worried though. She was worried about her mother, who'd taken to her bed with Mr Hardluck-Smythe's journal, while she waited for the pawn shop to open. She was worried about Cook breaking Sammy's crib. She was worried about Dog, who'd started licking tea stains off the rug, and about the stubborn emptiness of the Golden Jubilee biscuit tin. But her main source of anxiety was Captain Blunderfuss, who'd been gone a suspiciously long time. And when she heard a loud shriek from outside, she knew she'd been right to worry.

'Edward!' came Mrs Ponsonby-Smarm's panicked cry. 'There's a pirate in a flowery shawl crawling up our drainpipe. Are you listening to me, Edward? I said there's a villainous pirate on the loose, and he's heading for the bathroom. *Do* something, Edward.'

Odelia tore down the stairs and out into the early morning light, to find the lawn still full of treasure-hunting holes and a new hook-chopped gap in the bottom hedge. And on the other side of the gap stood Mrs Ponsonby-Smarm in her nightdress, pointing up at a familiar-looking pirate clinging on to her drainpipe for dear life.

'Captain?' called Odelia. 'What are you doing? I thought you said you were weeing in the flowerpots?

If it was a toilet you wanted, you could have used ours.'

'Weeing in the flowerpots?' repeated Mrs Ponsonby-Smarm, fanning herself with her hand. 'Heavens! Did you hear that, Edward?'

The drainpipe wobbled and creaked alarmingly as Captain Blunderfuss shook his head. 'It's diamonds I'm after, not a toilet. Those sparkly diamonds I spotted yesterday from the crow's nest window. I was going to prawn them for Sammy,' he added as if that made everything all right. 'Only I gots myself stuck on this silly rungless ladder, didn't I?'

Mrs Ponsonby's voice went up an octave. 'My diamonds?! Hurry Edward, fetch the police. Tell them there's a diamond-thieving pirate stuck up our drainpipe. A bloodthirsty criminal at large in Hadlington Gardens ... in a shawl.'

'No,' cried Odelia, thinking fast. 'You've got it all wrong. That's not a pirate, that's ... that's our window cleaner. He's a little eccentric, but he's *very* good at cleaning windows ... at making them sparkle like diamonds. He must have got confused and ended up at the wrong house. I'm so sorry for the disturbance.'

'A window cleaner?' repeated Mrs Ponsonby-Smarm.

'A widow cleaver?' snorted Captain Blunderfuss.
'You're the one who's confused, Basin. Stop your wiffle-
waffling and get me down from here. The diamonds
will have to wait … I think I *do* need a wee after all.'

'I'll fetch Cook,' Odelia called up to him. 'He'll
know what to do.'

She wasn't a hundred per cent sure Cook *would*
know how to remove a full-bladdered pirate from a
dangerously loose drainpipe, but she hurried back
through the gap in the hedge, hoping for the best.
Mrs Ponsonby-Smarm's voice carried after her: 'Just
when you think the Hardluck-Smythes can't lower the
tone of the neighbourhood any further, they go and get
themselves a filthy, smelly window cleaner who relieves
himself in people's flowerpots! Why, it makes me blush
just thinking about it. I've a good mind to go round
and see Mrs Hardluck-Smythe myself. Tell her that
widowhood is no excuse for such a blatant disregard
of decency and decorum …'

Huh! thought Odelia, as she dodged past the holes in the lawn and raced into the house. She didn't really know what decorum meant but it was very rude, nonetheless, of Mrs Ponsonby-Smarm to suggest that Mother had disregarded hers. Captain Blunderfuss might be a villainous varmint with bad breath and a terrible singing voice but, unlike their poisonous old bag of a next-door neighbour, at least he knew how to be nice to people. Actually, that wasn't strictly true, but the longer Odelia spent with him the more she'd come to realise that there was a good heart beating under his rough exterior.

'Cook!' she called, racing back up to the nursery to find him snoring in the crib. She shook the sleeping pirate by the shoulder. 'Wake up! The captain's in trouble.'

Cook stirred in his sleep, banging his head against the bars.

Odelia tried again. 'Please wake up. Captain Blunderfuss is stuck up next-door's drainpipe—'

She broke off at the sound of an almighty thump.

A thump, and a curse and a shrill cry of 'No! Not Father's precious Alpine Woodsia. My poor papa almost *died* getting that fern, you filthy good-for-nothing brute. He slipped off a foggy cliff in Wales, trying to complete his precious collection. And *now* look at it. Flattened. Absolutely *flattened.*'

'On second thoughts, don't worry,' Odelia told the still-snoring Cook. 'I think he's down now.' She hurried out to the landing window to see. Oh yes, Captain Blunderfuss was definitely down, and so was the Ponsonby-Smarms' drainpipe.

'His precious ants and woodworm, did you say?' came the pirate's booming voice as he picked himself up out of the neighbour's herbaceous border. 'Woodworm … yes, that's it!'

'No, his Alpine Woodsia,' repeated Mrs Ponsonby-Smarm, sounding more hysterical with every passing word. 'The one you've just crushed.'

But Captain Blunderfuss didn't seem to be listening. He was already speed-limping back towards the hedge. Already crawling through the hook-chopped gap and hurrying across the hole-strewn lawn … Odelia lost sight of him as he neared the house, but she could still hear his booming voice cutting through the early morning stillness.

'Bat bums and barnacles!' he bellowed. 'We forgot about the woodworm!'

Odelia frowned. Perhaps he'd hit his head when he landed. Perhaps the fall had scrambled his brains.

'I've got it, Basin!' came the captain's excited call from downstairs. 'I know how to find the nipper.'

You do? Odelia's heart leapt inside her chest. 'Where is he?' she cried. 'Where's Sammy? Tell me, Captain, pleeeeease.'

'Woodworm,' repeated Captain Blunderfuss. 'We just need to find the woodworm.'

CHAPTER 18

'We've been going about this all wrong,' explained the captain, sitting himself down at Mrs Hardluck-Smythe's mahogany writing desk. 'We shouldn't be scratching our beards over how to find the ram's bum money to pay those baby-stealing bandits. We need to find where they're keeping Sammy and steal him back again.'

'But how will we do that?' asked Odelia. 'We don't know which way they went once they left Birdcage

Walk. That's if they were ever there in the first place. I was only guessing that's where they meant.'

'But you think it was the woodworm man that took him?' said Captain Blunderfuss. 'The one who left the card that had you all worried.'

'Yes,' agreed Odelia. 'Mr Bugwell the woodworm man seemed exactly like the Admiral Arbuckle lookalike who followed us in the park. And they both match the policeman's description of the Mayfair Mob leader. I think they're all the same man.'

'Pre*slicely*,' said Captain Blunderfuss. 'So all we have to do …'

'is find the woodworm treatment services building,' finished Odelia. 'That must be where they're keeping Sammy! You're a genius, Captain.' She hurried off to retrieve the black-edged business card she'd hidden under her pillow the night before. *Don't worry, Sammy, we'll save you.*

Her heart was beating faster than ever as she raced back along the landing with the card clutched tight in her fist. 'Here it is! Look, there's an address at the bottom: 162 Waterloo Bridge Lane.'

'Then what are we waiting for?' said Captain Blunderfuss. 'Wake up, you drowsy dribble-head and fetch us some toast,' he added, poking Cook through the crib bars with Mrs Hardluck-Smythe's pearl-handled ink eraser. 'We've got a little feller to save.'

Breakfast was a sensible plan. Mr Hardluck-Smythe had always been a firm believer in the restorative powers of breakfast, claiming he was no good to anyone until he'd had his morning kippers. Yes, Odelia knew it made sense to get some proper food inside them – even if that food was only more toast – before they went charging off into the unknown. She knew they needed to keep their strength up for the dangers ahead. But it was hard to summon up much of an appetite with Sammy still missing and the grandfather clock ticking ever closer to their deadline.

Odelia fed her last few burnt bites to Dog while

the pirates weren't looking, and reclaimed her toasting fork, tucking it back into her ribbon belt in case of any fighting during their rescue mission. '*Now* can we go?' she begged, desperate to be on her way. She'd already scribbled a note for her mother, which she'd left on her desk:

Gone to rescue Sammy from woodworm.
Please don't worry.
Oddy x

She knew perfectly well that Mrs Hardluck-Smythe *would* worry though. She might even try and stop Odelia from going in the first place, which made a swift exit all the more important.

But at last Captain Blunderfuss declared himself full, 'although I could still do with some rum to wash it down,' and they were finally on their way, with Dog trotting down the road behind them.

The city was waking up again now. They hadn't even reached the end of Hadlington Gardens when a hansom cab came clattering towards them. Captain Blunderfuss leapt out into its path, just as he had the day before (although it seemed like half a lifetime ago now, to Odelia), and the cab came to a sharp halt.

'We need to get to Waterloo Bridge Lane,' Captain Blunderfuss shouted up to the driver – a grumpy-looking man with a dark beard and a bowler hat. His pirate hook caught on a wheel spoke as he hauled himself onto the passenger foot platform, and he almost fell back onto Odelia as she followed him up.

'What *are* you doing?' she hissed, keeping her voice low so the driver wouldn't hear through the trapdoor in the roof. 'We don't have any money to pay him.'

Captain Blunderfuss grinned. 'But we do have these,' he whispered, pulling a pair of Mr Hardluck-Smythe's silk bow ties out of his coat pocket. 'He'll just have to prawn them, won't he?'

Odelia wasn't sure cabmen took kindly to being paid in bow ties, but there was no time to argue. Cook was already climbing up behind her with Dog and soon all three of them were squeezed onto the two-person seat together. It would be much quicker than walking, Odelia told herself, and every second counted now.

'Ankles away!' Captain Blunderfuss called up to the driver.

'He means let's go,' explained Odelia.

Dog let out a hiss of fright as the cab rumbled off down the road, digging his claws into Odelia's bloomer-clad thighs.

'Shh,' said Cook, running his hand along the cat's fur. 'It's all right now. It's just like being at sea, only drier.'

It had been a long time since Odelia had ridden in a hansom cab. The experience was far bumpier than she remembered, and considerably smellier, although that might have had more to do with her travelling companions than the cab itself. She found herself sandwiched between Captain Blunderfuss's armpit and the filthy collar of Cook's food-encrusted shirt, which was *not* a very fragrant place to be. But despite the bumps and the smell, and the knot of nerves in her stomach, it felt good to be doing something, rather than sitting at home worrying about how they were going to raise the ransom money.

Odelia tried not to dwell on what the driver would say about paying their fare in bow ties, or how they'd save Sammy from a dangerous mob of thieves once they'd found him, by concentrating on the journey instead. She stared out at the smart-suited gentlemen on their way to their banks and offices, at the flower girls with their colourful posies fresh from the flower market at Covent Garden, and the shoeshine boys waiting with their brushes and blacking.

Every sight and sound brought back another memory of happier times. There was Mr Liberty's shop on Regent Street, where Mrs Hardluck-Smythe had ordered a new rug for Odelia's room. And there was the fancy tearoom, just off Piccadilly Circus, where Odelia's parents had taken her for pink-iced cakes after she'd recovered from the chickenpox. From her *varicella*. It was the grimy-faced children with pinched cheeks, searching for scraps in the gutters, who really caught her eye though … and the babies. Everywhere

Odelia looked she saw babies, from the china dolls in the toy shop to the blue-eyed cherubs on advertisements for soothing syrup; from the well-fed tot in her smart perambulator, out for an early morning stroll with her nanny, to the sickly-looking mite and his mother begging outside an inn. The knot of nerves in Odelia's stomach grew tighter with every infant they passed.

The carriage clattered on down Haymarket and onto Pall Mall, where an organ grinder's runaway monkey sent the horse (and carriage) skittering sideways, almost colliding with an omnibus coming the other way.

'This is the rottenest ship I've ever sailed on,' declared Captain Blunderfuss, clutching at his stomach in response to the sudden lurching movement. 'I'm sixteen shades of seasick here.' But he rallied enough to shout a passing insult at a man on a theatre poster, who bore an unfortunate resemblance to Admiral Arbuckle's second-in-command. He was still shouting when they reached Trafalgar Square, where Odelia and Mr Hardluck-Smythe used to admire the paintings in The National Gallery. And he was *still* shouting as

Odelia bent forwards in her seat for a closer look at Nelson on his tall stone column. There was something about the shape of the statue's hat that had always reminded her of a pirate, and she seemed to remember her father telling her that Nelson had lost an eye too. Or was that an arm?

'Look,' she said, hoping to distract the captain by pointing out a fellow seaman. 'That's Admiral Lord Nelson, hero of the British Navy.'

'*Admiral Smellson?* Earwigs and apple sauce,' cursed the pirate, leaning out of the carriage to glare at the statue. 'I *hate* admirals. Shove off, you stony stinkfish!' he roared, sending a gentleman in a top hat toppling backwards into the fountain in surprise. Dog seemed equally unimpressed with the stone lions, his mangy white fur standing on end as he hissed at them. As for Cook, he'd fallen asleep again, snoring away like a pig as his head slumped sideways onto Odelia's shoulder.

Odelia's chest tightened as the murky brown waters of the Thames came into view. She was thinking of those fateful words in her father's diary: *Perhaps a ride along the Thames will help clear my head and shift this wretched cold …* She was thinking of his final moments, flying over the handlebars of his safety bicycle towards the dark chill of the river and the hard prow of the waiting coal barge. *But today isn't a day for tears,* she told herself firmly. Today Odelia Harmony Hardluck-Smythe was a sub-ordinary, second-in-commode, ship's basin pirate, and pirates with such long titles never cried. Especially not when they had baby brothers to save.

'Look, there's Cleopatra's Needle,' she said as they turned onto the Embankment, pointing towards the famous Egyptian column.

'Cleopatra's seagulls?' repeated Captain Blunderfuss, craning his neck out of the carriage for a better view. 'More like Cleopatra's albatrosses.'

What? Odelia was confused for a moment. *What do albatrosses have to do with anything?* And then – as the cab turned onto Waterloo Bridge, with its beautiful granite arches – she saw them: a flock of giant seabirds circling around the domed roof of St Paul's Cathedral. Could they be the albatrosses from Mrs Hardluck-Smythe's book? Had the peculiar writing magic worked after all? They weren't attacking anyone, admittedly (thank goodness!) but Odelia had never heard of albatrosses in London before. That had to mean something.

As the cab clattered across the bridge, with the full majesty of the Thames spread out before them, Odelia's thoughts turned to the five hundred pounds Mrs Hardluck-Smythe had written into the biscuit tin. Would that have magically appeared by now too? For a moment she let herself imagine what they'd do with the money if they didn't need it for Sammy's ransom any more. If she and the pirates managed to save him without paying Mr Bugwell his five hundred pounds. They'd need to replace the Ponsonby-Smarm's hedge and drainpipe, of course. And then there was the promised charitable donation to help the homeless. That still left a small fortune though, for new clothes ... for proper food that *wasn't* toast ... for family holidays at the seaside with Sammy... Not that Odelia cared about any of that, as long as they had Sammy back safe and sound. *We're coming*, she promised him silently. *We're almost there.*

Odelia jumped as the driver pulled on his lever to open the trapdoor above their heads. 'This is Waterloo Bridge Lane,' he called down through the gap. 'What number did you want?'

'One hundred and sixty-two,' Odelia called back.

'There *is* no number one hundred and sixty-two,' came the reply. 'It only goes up to forty.'

CHAPTER 19

'I must have made a mistake. Perhaps I misremembered,' said Odelia, pulling Mr Bugwell's business card out of her shirt pocket to check. But there was no mistake: 162 Waterloo Bridge Lane. She tried a different tack. 'It's the Waterloo Woodworm Treatment Services building – *that's* where we need to go.'

'Never heard of it,' said the driver. 'You'll have to get out here and look for it yourself. That'll be two shillings and sixpence thank you.'

'No,' said Captain Blunderfuss. 'That'll be two bow ties and *no* pence.'

The driver cleared his throat, ready to argue, but soon thought better of it when Captain Blunderfuss thrust his hook up through the trapdoor. 'Two bow ties it is, sir. I'll be wishing you all a good day then.'

Captain Blunderfuss turned to Odelia with a grin, as the cab clattered off into the distance. 'You see, Basin? I told you it would be all right.'

Odelia nodded, but the sinking sensation in her stomach felt far from all right. There *was* no Waterloo Woodworm Treatment Services, was there? The address was as fake as Mr Bugwell's offer of a no-obligation examination of the house. She should have guessed. The Mayfair Mob were a master criminal gang. Why would they give out business cards telling everyone where to find them?

A thorough search of all the properties along Waterloo Bridge Lane and the surrounding roads did little to lift Odelia's spirits. There were no signs of any woodworm specialists. No sign of Mr Bugwell and his gang of thieves. And no sign of Sammy. *Oh Sammy, where are you?*

'This was a stupid idea,' Odelia said angrily, as Cook stopped to wipe horse dung off his boot. 'I should never have listened to you,' she told Captain Blunderfuss. 'I should never have come. I should have stayed at home with Mother and concentrated on finding the ransom money instead.' But then she saw the hurt look on the captain's face and her anger melted away again as quickly as it had arrived. 'I'm sorry,' she said. 'I didn't mean it. I'm just worried about Sammy, that's all. I'd be lost without you. You're the best thing that's happened to me in a very long time.'

Captain Blunderfuss blushed as he shook his head. 'Aw, stop it now, you're making my eyeball water.' He pulled out his filthy handkerchief and dabbed at his cheek.

'How can a captain like me be glum,' he sang softly.
'With velvet trousers on my pirate bum,
And warm toasty feelings in my pirate chest?
'Cos my trusty Basin, she's the best.'

Odelia was the one blushing now.

Captain Blunderfuss reached towards her with his hook and lifted a stray strand of hair away from her eyes. And then he grinned. 'Well, don't just stand there roasting your face-cheeks, let's get home and work on that ram's bum.'

'Aye aye, Captain. Wait, what happened to Cook and Dog?' Odelia asked, turning round to find them gone.

'I think they're hiding from the albatross,' said Captain Blunderfuss.

'What albatross?' Odelia looked up to see a giant bird with a white stomach and enormous, black-topped wings swooping down out of the sky. 'Oh, *that* albatross.' She ducked as a sharp beak lunged at her head. 'Would you say it's attacking us?'

Captain Blunderfuss waved his hook at the bird nd roared. 'Pick on someone your own size, you feathery fart-face! No one pecks *my* basin and gets away with it.' He turned back to Odelia. 'Yes, I'd call this an attack.'

'Excellent,' said Odelia, a fresh flicker of hope

flaring inside of her. 'Mother's writing magic must have worked.' She ducked into a nearby doorway as the albatross swooped back down a second time. 'With any luck there'll be a full biscuit tin of money waiting for us by the time we get home.'

The journey back home was an altogether slower, more wearying affair. By the time Captain Blunderfuss and Odelia had seen off the albatross and tracked down Cook (who'd been sleeping off his fear behind a wall, with Dog as a furry, purry blanket), Big Ben was already chiming ten o'clock. And by the time the pirate crew had wound their way back across London on foot, stopping en route to rescue a rat-chasing Dog from an open coal chute, the grandfather clock was chiming eleven. Only seven more hours to go.

'You didn't find him then?' said Mrs Hardluck-Smythe, who'd been pacing up and down the hall waiting for their return.

Odelia shook her head. 'No, I'm sorry. It turned out to be a false start. But we *did* get attacked by an albatross.'

'Gracious me,' said her mother. 'Are you all right?'

'Yes,' said Odelia. 'We made a catapult out of Captain Blunderfuss's eyepatch and my lucky marble. I got the idea from your book – from the extra bit you were writing last night. And it worked!'

'Thank heavens.'

'And I don't just mean the catapult. I mean your *book* worked. The *magic* worked. That must be where the albatrosses came from. Which means the biscuit tin must have worked too. It must be full of money by now.' Odelia raced up to the nursery to see. There was the Golden Jubilee tin, waiting on her mother's desk beside a pawnbroker's ticket for one gold wedding ring.

Please let the money be here. Please, please, please …

Odelia opened up the tin with trembling fingers and gasped out loud.

CHAPTER 20

The tin was empty.

It was still empty when she checked again at 11.30.

It was still empty at midday.

'I could ask Mr Pickfill if he'd accept a half-written pirate book for an advance of five hundred pounds,' said Mrs Hardluck-Smythe, but there was little hope in her eyes as she said it. There was even less hope in her eyes when she returned home an hour later with a resounding 'no' from Mr Pickfill's secretary and an advance of no pounds whatsoever.

'I could have another try at getting those sparkly diamonds from Mrs Poisonous-Smarm,' suggested Captain Blunderfuss.

'I could make some toast to sell,' offered Cook. 'Or hire Dog out as a rat-catcher?'

Odelia shook her head. 'There's *got* to be a better plan than that.' She gave the biscuit tin another shake while she was at it, still hoping to hear something soft and papery rattling around inside ... 'Something soft and papery,' she whispered to herself. The tin was empty – she didn't even need to open it to know that – but she *could* feel the start of an idea rattling round in her brain. 'Something soft ... and papery ... Yes!' she cried. 'That's it! I know how to get Sammy back. I know what we need to do.'

'Is it hand-to-hook combat?' Captain Blunderfuss asked. 'Take that, you scurvy scoundrels. Unhand that baby and get ready to walk the plank.'

'No,' said Odelia. 'We don't want any fighting.'

'Wait, I know, harpoons! That'll show 'em. Take

that, you stinking–'

'NO,' cut in Odelia. 'It's not *any* of those things. We're going to stick to Plan A. We're going to write ourselves some money. Only I don't mean in a book, I mean in real life. We'll make our *own* notes. Five hundred pounds' worth. And then even if the writing magic *doesn't* work in time, we've still got a chance.'

'We're going to *forge* money, you mean?' asked Mrs Hardluck-Smythe.

'Exactly. I doubt it will fool them for long, but that's all right. Once we've got Sammy back safe and sound we can–'

'FIGHT THEM!' roared the pirate, swishing his hook through the air like a sword.

'Make a run for it,' finished Odelia. 'But if it comes to it, yes, I suppose we'll fight them. You get Sammy to safety,' she told her mother, 'and we'll take care of the thieves.'

Mrs Hardluck-Smythe looked more doubtful than ever.

'It's not the *best* plan,' Odelia admitted. 'But it

beats climbing up drainpipes in search of diamonds or selling toast on the street. And at least we'll be doing *something*. I'll help with drawing the crests, and Captain Blunderfuss can cut up the paper and make it look old and grubby.'

'Aye aye, Basin. There's no one better than me when it comes to cutting,' boasted the pirate, giving his hook another swoosh. '*Or* at making things grubby.'

Mrs Hardluck-Smythe took a deep breath and nodded. 'All right then. Let's do it.'

'What about me?' asked Cook. 'What shall I do?'

'What you do best, of course,' said Odelia.

'Sleeping?'

'No, I meant cooking.' Odelia handed him her trusty toasting fork. 'We're going to need a big pile of toast to keep us going while we work. And nobody burns it better than you.'

Cook grinned. 'Aye aye, Basin. One pile of burnt toast coming right up.'

Forging money turned out to be a lot harder than Odelia had expected. She stared in dismay at the spreading sea of ten pound notes drying on the nursery floor, willing them to turn into real money. But the longer she sat there staring at them, the more fake and phoney they seemed. Captain Blunderfuss had done an excellent job at cutting them to size and making them look grubby – Odelia wasn't sure she wanted to know *how* he'd made them so dirty, exactly – but Mrs Hardluck-Smythe's penmanship and her own artwork left a lot to be desired.

Ringworm and ruination! These won't fool anyone, Odelia thought, imagining the look of fury on Mr Bugwell's face when he opened up the biscuit tin and found nothing but slips of paper inside. Dirty slips of paper with ink-splotted text and wonky crests. *How will we ever get Sammy back then?* She imagined the look of delight on her brother's face when she appeared – Oddy! Oddy piwate! – turning to confusion and fear as the thieves refused to hand him over. As they carried him away to … to … No, she couldn't bear to think what they'd do to him when they realised they'd been tricked. Oh Sammy. Dear, sweet little Sammy.

If only Odelia knew how the magic worked – the strange writing magic that had brought Captain Blunderfuss blundering into their lives and made the treasure map appear in his pocket out of nowhere. That had brought a flock of albatrosses all the way to the Thames. But no matter how many times she checked inside the biscuit tin, hoping and wishing and squeezing her lucky marble tight, it was still empty. And now it was almost four o'clock, and Captain Blunderfuss had disappeared off in search of more food, leaving Cook asleep on the landing floor and Odelia and her mother alone in a drying sea of fake bank notes.

The sound of the backless grandfather clock striking the hour reverberated all the way up the stairs and in through the open nursery door.

Bong … bong … bong … Odelia counted up the chimes as she scooped the finished notes into a neat pile, each 'bong' bringing her closer to their appointment with the thieves.

Bong ... four o'clock! Only two more hours to wait now. Two more hours to save Sammy.

Bong!

What? That sounded like five chimes. No, there had to be a mistake. She must have miscounted.

But she hadn't.

'Five o'clock?' cried Mrs Hardluck-Smythe, who'd clearly lost track of the time as well. 'Oh heavens! That'll have to do,' she added, dashing off a wiggly cashier's signature in the bottom corner of her final note. 'We have to get ready. We can't be late. Where's Captain Blunderfuss?'

'He went to get some toast, I think ... something to do with a rumbling tummy. Don't worry – he can't have gone far. I'll tell him to hurry up.'

Odelia raced down to the kitchen – the empty kitchen. There was no sign of any pirate activity. No sign of any toast. Just the open back door, swaying lightly on its hinges in the late afternoon breeze. *Oh no*, Odelia thought. *Please tell me he hasn't gone back for Mrs Ponsonby-Smarm's diamond necklace?*

'Captain!' she called, heading out into the garden in her stockinged feet. 'Captain Blunderfuss!'

'Help! Thief!' came a shrill answering cry. A posh, outraged kind of cry.

But it wasn't diamonds Mrs Ponsonby-Smarm's thief had come for this time.

'Come back with our carp, you filthy fish-stealing villain!'

Oh no. Not again.

'I didn't steal *nothing*, you fish-counting cod-face,' came the pirate's reply, as Odelia raced across the lawn towards the gap in the hedge. 'I *collected* them. It's not stealing if they swim into your hat, fairs and squares. That's *asking* to be eaten, that is.'

'*Eaten?!* You're not a window cleaner at all, are you? You're a drainpipe-breaking, hedge-hacking, fish-stealing *pirate*,' came Mrs Ponsonby-Smarm's hysterical cry, as Odelia scrambled through the hedge to find her neighbour wearing a blue taffeta dress and a look of outrage. And there was Captain Blunderfuss, back in his own coat again, cradling his upturned tricorn hat in his arms like a bowl. A bowl of fish, presumably. 'Good heavens, Edward!' continued Mrs Ponsonby-Smarm. 'Did you hear that? He's eating our precious carp! Are you listening to me, Edward? I said that villainous pirate from next door is stealing our fish in his filthy hat and cooking them up for tea!'

'Yes, dear, I heard you loud and clear, thank you very much,' came her husband's weary reply from inside the house. Mr Hardluck-Smythe used to say that the real reason Edward Ponsonby-Smarm spent such long hours at his law offices was because he'd rather be working than at home listening to his dreadful nag of a wife. 'I'm sure the whole of Hadlington Gardens heard you.'

'Well do something then. Fetch the police for goodness' sake. The man's a menace to polite society.'

'No, please don't bring the police into this,' Odelia begged. 'There's no need for that. It's a misunderstanding, that's all. I'm sure the captain's very sorry and he's going to put your fish back in the pond now. *Aren't you?*'

'I can't be expected to fight on an empty stomach,'

grumbled the pirate, still clinging to his hat. 'It'd be different if I had my own cannon …'

'I said you're going to put the fish back now, *aren't* you, Captain?'

'But …'

'We haven't got time for this,' Odelia told him sternly. 'If we're not at the Hyde Park bandstand by six o'clock, it's *all* over.'

'But … but …'

'Buttercups and bin lids,' she said. 'Come on, let's go.'

'Fine,' said the pirate grudgingly, scooping the carp out one by one and tossing them at Odelia's horrified next-door neighbour. 'Have your stupid fish back. That last one I had was full of marbles anyway.'

CHAPTER 21

The bandstand, which had been moved from Kensington Gardens a few years before to its current spot in Hyde Park, just up from the big bronze statue of Achilles, had always been a happy place for Odelia. It was a place of cheerful afternoon concerts and chattering crowds, of cooling ginger beer or cucumber ice cream and her father's smartly booted feet tapping along in time to the beat. There was no noisy brass band playing polkas or arrangements of opera arias today though. No crowds. No happiness. No Father. Just a tummyful of nerves and a biscuit tin of forged money. Odelia checked the tin one last time as the bandstand's octagonal roof loomed into view through the early evening fog, but the fake notes were as fake as ever.

'I'll take that now, thank you,' said Mrs Hardluck-Smythe, as Odelia replaced the lid. 'I think it's best if I meet the thieves on my own.'

'But …'

'I need you to stay out of the way,' her mother told her. 'Stay safe. That's *your* job.'

'But …' *But what if it goes wrong? What if there's fighting?* Odelia felt for the toasting fork tucked into her ribbon belt.

'I mean it, Oddy. I've already lost one of my children and I'm not going to risk losing another. You stay here with Cook and the captain and leave the negotiations to me. Then once we've done the handover, you take Sammy and run. You'll be faster than me. Whatever happens just keep running. Don't so much as turn around until you're home safely. Got it?'

'But … but …'

'Butterscotch and bumblebees,' finished Mrs Hardluck-Smythe, stroking Odelia's face with ink-stained fingers. 'I know I haven't been the best mother lately, darling. I've been too wrapped up in my own worries and grief, haven't I? In my books. But I love you so very much. You and Sammy really are the most precious treasure anyone could ask for – your father was quite right about that. My glittering jewels to brighten the darkest of dark days. Yes,' she said, planting a kiss on her daughter's forehead. 'Even in the midst of all our misfortune, I'm still the luckiest woman alive.'

'Flibbering fleabites, you're making my eyeball water again,' complained the pirate, dabbing at his cheek with his handkerchief. 'What kind of battle talk is that? What happened to making our enemies walk the plank and feeding them to the sharks?'

Mrs Hardluck-Smythe took no notice. 'Things are going to be different from now on though,' she promised. 'Once Sammy's back safe and sound, we're going to be a *proper* family again, bills or no bills. And if I can't find a better way of making ends meet, I'll just have to …'

'Rob the bossy old bag next door?' suggested Captain Blunderfuss. 'Get a job in a marzipan fruit factory?'

'I don't know, exactly, but I'll think of somethi–' Mrs Hardluck-Smythe broke off at the sound of voices approaching through the mist.

'Dada!' came a distant cry.

'Quick, get back behind that bush,' ordered Mrs Hardluck-Smythe. 'Look after my precious daughter, Captain, I'm going in …'

Odelia could do nothing but watch, her heart hammering triple time, as her brave mother climbed the bandstand steps with a biscuit tin of badly forged ten pound notes; as dark looming shapes emerged from a clump of trees on the other side. She pulled her lucky marble from her shirt pocket and squeezed it tight.

'Mama!' called Sammy. 'Mama piwate!'

'Yes, Mummy's here, Sammy,' Mrs Hardluck-Smythe called back, her voice impressively firm and steady. 'But there's no pirate, only me. I'm completely alone.'

'And you've brought the money?' called someone else. A deep-voiced, well-spoken sort of someone.

'Mr Bugwell,' whispered Odelia, reaching for her trusty toasting fork. Just in case. Although now that they were here, the idea of actually *fighting* anyone with it made her feel queasy inside.

'Admiral Arbuckle,' hissed Captain Blunderfuss, polishing the end of his hook on his coat tails. 'I should have known. If he's hurt so much as a single hair on that little feller's head, I'll ... I'll ...'

'Yes, the money's all here,' said Mrs Hardluck-Smythe, rattling the biscuit tin as if to prove it. A tall, elegant figure stepped up onto the bandstand beside her. 'Five hundred pounds, as agreed. Give me back my baby boy and it's all yours.'

'Money first,' insisted Mr Bugwell. 'I need to check it's all there, don't I? Make sure there hasn't been any funny business.'

Odelia gulped. Funny business didn't *get* much funnier than hand-forging five hundred pounds and passing them off as ransom money.

Mrs Hardluck-Smythe held her ground though. 'That's all very well,' she said. 'But how do I know I can trust *you*? How about you give me Sammy and I'll give you your money at the same time?'

'Very well,' agreed Mr Bugwell. 'But if you try anything, there'll be trouble, got it? There are six of us, and only one of you, so you'd better do as you're told … or else.'

There it was again – that 'or else', just like in the ransom note. Odelia *still* didn't know what it meant, exactly, but she was more certain than ever that she didn't want to find out. *Please let the magic work*, she begged, squeezing her lucky marble even tighter. *Please let the money have changed in time. Or else …*

Five more tall, shadowy figures climbed up the steps onto the bandstand as Odelia watched in breath-held fear from behind the bush. Five tall figures and one wiggling bundle of baby brother.

'Mama! Mama bic bic!' cried Sammy, catching sight of the biscuit tin as the other thieves passed him over to Mr Bugwell.

'Sammy!' Mrs Hardluck-Smythe let out a strangled sob. 'Oh Sammy!' For a moment she appeared lost for words – too overcome by emotion to keep going any longer. But then she seemed to pull herself together again, forcing a brittle brightness back into her voice. 'Don't worry,' she told him. 'Everything's going to be all right. Mummy's going to give these nice gentlemen their money, and then take you home for some toast.'

'What will he do when he finds out we tricked him?' Odelia whispered. She could hardly bear to watch.

'He won't be doing nothing,' said Captain Blunderfuss, readjusting his hat. ' 'Cause the moment they hand over the little feller, we get 'em.'

'Get them? What do you mean?' That *wasn't* part of Mrs Hardluck-Smythe's plan. There'd been no mention of 'getting' anyone.

'I mean we get 'em,' repeated the pirate. 'Nab 'em. Bosh 'em. Squish 'em. Squash 'em. Buckle their swashes and scuttle their butts.'

'Oh. I see.' Odelia couldn't decide which was more scary. Staying and watching helplessly, as per her mother's instructions, or charging headfirst into a gang of criminals with nothing but a toasting fork by way of a weapon.

'You leave Admiral Arbuckle to me though,' added Captain Blunderfuss, pointing at Mr Bugwell. 'Me and him have got unfinished business. Any of the others is fair game, mind.'

Odelia shivered. Was now a good time to admit that she'd never fought anything more dangerous than a fly before? That it would take more than a pair of bloomers and an oversized shirt to turn her into a proper pirate? She wasn't a sub-ordinary *or* a basin, she realised as she cowered behind the bush, her courage slipping away quicker than you could say 'I think I've changed my mind'. She was just a regular eleven-year-old girl, playing at dress-up and treasure-hunting to try and fill the aching emptiness inside. And five tall thieves against one terrified girl with a toasting fork, and a sleepy cook with one ear, didn't seem like a fair battle somehow. Certainly not one they had any chance of winning.

'Oh yes, we've unfinished business all right,' continued Captain Blunderfuss with an angry growl. 'Fifteen chapters of unfinished business, according to your mother, plus some *very* rude comments about the state of my trousers.'

'The thing is,' Odelia began. 'I've never actually *done* any fighting before, unless you count …'

But Captain Blunderfuss wasn't listening. 'Here we go,' he said, his gaze firmly fixed on the bandstand. 'Get ready …'

'On the count of three,' called Mrs Hardluck-Smythe.

'On *my* count of three, you mean,' replied Mr Bugwell, taking hold of Sammy.

'On three,' hissed Captain Blunderfuss.

'Wee-wee!' cried Sammy.

'Pigfish …' Odelia clutched at her toasting fork with sweat-slippery fingers. 'Pigfish and … and …' But her words seemed to have escaped along with the last of her courage. She couldn't even finish her own curses now.

'One …' counted everyone together.

I don't think I can do this.

'Two …'

I shouldn't even be here.

'Thr–'

'There he is!' cried Mrs Ponsonby-Smarm, breaking through the line of trees and charging across the neatly cut grass with a pair of helmeted policemen panting at her side. 'That's the villain who stole our fish. I told you they were headed for the bandstand.' And then suddenly everyone was shouting at once.

'Seize him!'

'Get 'em!'

'Stop her!'

'Sammy!'

'Wee-wee!'

'Help!'

'Three!' Captain Blunderfuss was already off, hobbling up to the bandstand with impressive speed, while Odelia looked on in shock.

Boof! Mrs Hardluck-Smythe walloped Mr Bugwell over the head with the biscuit tin. The lid flew off on impact, sending fake ten pound notes fluttering through the air, as Mrs Hardluck-Smythe attempted to wrestle her son out of the thief's arms.

'No police, I said,' he screamed at her, refusing to relinquish his prize.

'Nothing to do with *me*,' Mrs Hardluck-Smythe screamed back, aiming a very unladylike knee at his velvet-clad gentleman's particulars.

Bam!

'Owwwwwwwwwww!' Mr Bugwell doubled over in pain, loosening his grip on Sammy enough for Mrs Hardluck-Smythe to snatch him away.

'Mama! Mama badda wee-wee!'

'Oh Sammy, my darling!'

'Don't just stand there,' squealed Mr Bugwell. 'Seize them.'

'Don't just stand there,' shouted Odelia, as her mother hugged Sammy tight. 'Run!'

'Oddy! Oddy piwate!'

'Run, Mother,' Odelia shouted again, as Mrs Hardluck-Smythe clattered down the bandstand steps with Sammy clutched to her chest and the other thieves in hot pursuit. And then somehow Odelia found that *she* was running too, her toasting fork held high in front of her like a sword. 'Pigfish and poppycock,' she roared as she ran. Only it wasn't a curse any more. It was a battle cry. She glanced up to find Cook at her side, still wearing his shawl but looking more awake than she'd ever seen him before, with Dog tearing along behind him … and then … well, it was hard to tell *what* was happening in the wild tangle of arms and legs and white furry tails. Of hooks and claws and truncheons and swinging toasting forks …

'Oof!'

'Ow!'

'Miaow!'

'Watch it!'

'Take that, you smarm-faced trouser show-off!'

'Grab him!'

'Stop them!'

'How's this for chapter sixteen then, you puffed-up peacock? How d'you like *this* plot twist?'

'Dada! Dada piwate!'

'Oddy? Where's my Oddy? Unhand me, you ruffian.'

Smack. Clatter. Bash.

'Get this filthy cat off my face!'

'Oddy! Oddy badda bam bam!'

'Let go of her now, or I'll beat you like an egg. I'll whip you like cream. I'll mash you like spuds.'

'That's him, Officer,' called Mrs Ponsonby-Smarm across the struggle. 'That's the no-good villain who stole our prized fish. He wants locking up and …'

BREEEEEEEEEEEP! A shrill whistle cut through the noise and chaos. *BREEEP BREEEEP BREEEEEP!*

'THAT'S ENOUGH,' roared an extra-important-looking policeman with extra-bushy eyebrows. 'EVERYONE FREEZE.'

CHAPTER 22

Odelia froze.

The thief she was fighting froze.

Even Mr Bugwell, swinging off the pirate's hook by the collar of his fancy jacket, froze.

'Now then,' said the important-looking policeman with the bushy eyebrows, prodding Mr Bugwell with his finger. 'What do we have here then?'

'That's the leader of the Mayfair Mob,' said Odelia, slipping her weapon back into her belt in case there was a law against using toasting forks in a public park. 'The one you've all been looking for. He and his gang broke into our house and stole my baby brother. We're just here to get him back, with the help of our butler,' she said, pointing to Captain Blunderfuss. 'And our cook,' she added, pointing to Cook, who'd wrestled one of the thieves to the bandstand floor and was using his stomach as a pillow for his boots. Dog, meanwhile, had decided to use the thief's *face* as a pillow and was curled up in a cosy ball, purring happily.

'Don't be ridiculous,' said Mr Bugwell, struggling to unhook himself. 'I'm a respectable law-abiding citizen going about my early evening walk. Or at least I *was*, until this bumptious buccaneer attacked me.'

'Too right I attacked you,' agreed Captain Blunderfuss. 'Turns out *you* were the baddy all along and I'm the hero.'

'Well, I wouldn't say *hero* exactly …' began Mrs Hardluck-Smythe. But then she stopped and corrected herself. 'Actually, no, you're right. You *are* a hero, Captain. Dashing in here to help save Sammy. Catching the leader of the Mayfair Mob single-handedly. I'm sorry about your other hand,' she added, 'I really am, but you have to admit your hook does have its uses.'

'You saved me too,' said Odelia. 'I was miserable before you came. We all were. And now look at us. Fighting thieves in the park! Buckling their swashes and scuttling their butts.'

The important-looking policeman stared at Mr Bugwell – a long, detecting kind of stare – and then pulled out his notebook. 'Let's see now ... tall, handsome and elegant ... yes, that sounds about right ... with a long, pointy nose, dark glittering eyes and a fine line in green velvet trousers. Tick, tick and tick. Looks and sounds like a proper gentleman ... spot on, I'd say. Arrest this man at once,' he called to his officers, unhooking Mr Bugwell and tugging his hands behind his back.

'And them,' said Odelia, pointing to the other thieves. 'They're all in it together. You need to arrest them too.'

Mr Bugwell scowled. 'Preposterous! *They're* the ones

that want locking up – that filthy pirate and his no-good crew.'

'A pirate?' exclaimed Mrs Hardluck-Smythe. 'In Mayfair? *Now* who's being preposterous? Captain Blunderfuss is the finest of butlers.'

'He's a no-good villain who stole our fish, you mean,' cut in Mrs Ponsonby-Smarm. '*And* flattened my Alpine Woodsia.'

'The captain didn't steal your fish,' said Odelia, thinking quickly. 'He was just rescuing my lucky marble for me. Which means the *fish* was the thief, really, for swallowing it in the first place and …'

But the important-looking policeman had stopped listening. He was too busy scooping up soggy ten pound notes from the bandstand floor. Too busy raising his bushy eyebrows and pursing his lips in a crime-detecting sort of way. 'Well, well, well,' he said. 'And what do we have *here*? It looks like we've got ourselves a bank forger too.'

No, thought Odelia. *Jellied eels and jam jars! This can't be happening.*

But it was.

'Forged?' repeated Mr Bugwell. 'You mean the money is fake?'

The policeman nodded. 'And a very *bad* fake at that. But that doesn't make it any less of a crime.'

'It was her,' shrieked Mr Bugwell, jabbing his finger at Mrs Hardluck-Smythe. 'You can't pin that one on me. She had a whole biscuit tin full of them. *She's* the real criminal round here.'

'Mama!' agreed Sammy. 'Mama bic bic!'

Mrs Hardluck-Smythe had turned deathly pale. 'But ... but ...'

'Buttlescuts and blowfish,' finished Captain Blunderfuss, laying a grubby but gentle hand on her arm. 'I've got this. It was me what did it, Mr Policeman. Forking that money, I mean. I'm the one that wants locking up.'

'No, Captain,' said Mrs Hardluck-Smythe. 'I can't let you ...'

'You're too late, Mrs Writer-Lady. I already have. You take care of the little feller and my trusty basin and let me take care of this. And Cook?'

Cook opened a sleepy eye and nodded. 'Aye, Captain?'

'If you make it back to *The Sea Lion's Bellybutton*, help yourself to some of my rum. You've earned it.'

There were tears in Odelia's eyes and a lump in her throat as Captain Blunderfuss was carted away in hook-and-handcuffs. She'd been hoping they'd take him to the local police station right there in Hyde Park, but she was out of luck. Perhaps the cells were already full. Or perhaps the important-looking policeman had somewhere even more secure in mind for a dangerous, money-forging pirate and the infamous Mayfair Mob. Odelia could only watch and weep as they bundled her beloved captain off like a common criminal.

It was a sad, sorry party that headed home afterwards, pushing through the crowd of curious onlookers who'd gathered at the scene – a mix of well-to-do folk on their evening promenade and poor, penniless vagrants – and winding their way back along the Serpentine towards Hadlington Gardens. It wasn't the quickest or the most direct way home – far from it, in fact – but Odelia wanted to remember the adventures she'd shared there.

'That's where Captain Blunderfuss took us fishing,' she said, pointing to a seemingly random spot along the bank, halfway between Serpentine Island and the bridge. She sighed. There was nothing remarkable about that particular stretch of bank – nothing to mark it out from any other stretch – but it was special to Odelia. She could still see the pirate pouring fish out of his makeshift veil-net into Sammy's perambulator. So many fish! She could still picture the dandruff flakes on his shoulder as they leant over the treasure map together. So many flakes!

'Dada piwate spwat!' cried Sammy, kicking his legs in excitement, as if he was remembering it too. 'Spwat, spwat, spwat!'

Oh Captain! What will I do without you? 'And that's where the thief was sitting,' Odelia added, pointing to the nearby bench. 'If only I'd kept my mouth shut about the treasure being at our house, none of this would ever have happened. Captain Blunderfuss would still be here.' She thought of his final act of bravery – the way he gave himself up to save their family – and her heart squeezed tight inside her ribs. 'What will happen to him, Mother? What's the punishment for forging money?'

'I dread to think.' The colour had come back to Mrs Hardluck-Smythe's cheeks now, but her voice was quiet and quavery. 'Hopefully he'll disappear back into his story instead. Yes,' she said, sounding sadder than ever. 'That'll be the best thing for everyone.'

Best for Captain Blunderfuss, thought Odelia – *better than rotting in jail, anyway* – but not better for her. Or Sammy. It felt like losing Father all over again. Even Mother had grown fond of him in her own way – which wasn't so surprising, really, given that she was the one who'd created him in the first place. 'Couldn't you just *write* him out of jail? Maybe you could slip a key into his pocket or something?'

'Like the money, you mean? We all know how *that*

turned out.'

Oh yes, the money, thought Odelia, with another pang of guilt. That was all her fault too. It had been her idea to write the money into the tin by magic. Her idea to fake the notes instead. It should be *her* behind bars, not the pirate. *What kind of basin abandons her brave captain at the first sign of trouble?*

'It's no good,' she cried. 'We can't leave him to take all the blame. I need to tell the police what *really* happened. I need to make things right. Here, take this,' Odelia said, sliding the toasting fork back out of her belt and handing it to Cook for safekeeping – and toast-making. 'Look after Mother and Sammy for me.'

'Aye aye, Basin,' said Cook solemnly, with an equally solemn miaow from Dog.

'Don't worry. There'll be no fighting this time,' Odelia told Mrs Hardluck-Smythe. 'Just the truth.'

Mrs Hardluck-Smythe shook her head. 'But … but …'

'Buttonholes and baby smiles,' replied Odelia, kissing Sammy goodbye. 'Wish me luck!'

'Oddy, no, don't be ridiculous,' called Mrs Hardluck-Smythe. 'Come back!'

But it was too late.

'Batten down the hatches and hoist the mainsail, Captain,' Odelia called as she tore back through the park. 'I'm on my way.'

News must have got out already. By the time Odelia found the right police station – after two false starts and a long detour round half of Knightsbridge – the front steps of the imposing, stone-fronted building were thronging with people hoping for a glimpse of the famous Mayfair Mob. Or maybe it was the money-forging pirate they'd come to see. Top hats and bowlers jostled for position with posh, flowery bonnets, flat caps and bare heads. People from every walk of life, it seemed, had gathered for a gawp. There were even a couple of newspaper reporters there, notebooks at the ready to catch all the details.

'Sorry,' said Odelia, pushing a path through the jutting elbows and full skirts towards the blue police lamp hanging by the front door. 'Excuse me, please.'

'Oh no you don't,' snapped a pink-hatted lady at the bottom of the steps, batting at Odelia's shins with her rolled-up parasol. 'We were here first. If you want to see the bloodthirsty baby-stealing pirate on his way to jail, you'll have to wait your turn.'

'What? No,' said Odelia. '*He* didn't steal the baby. He helped save him. And he's not bloodthirsty, he's just a bit rough round the edges, that's all.'

'I heard he killed four policemen with his nasty big hook,' piped up the red-nosed man behind her. 'That certainly sounds bloodthirsty to me.'

'Well, *I* heard he held up a bank with a toasting fork and stole five hundred pounds,' said his neighbour, a scowling man with grey mutton chops.

'Don't be ridiculous,' said someone else. 'It wasn't a bank, it was a biscuit factory.'

'You're *all* wrong,' cried Odelia. 'He didn't kill

anyone, and he didn't steal any money either. Or biscuits. The police think he forged some banknotes – *that's* why they arrested him – but they've got it wrong too. Captain Blunderfuss might look and sound like a varmint, but deep down he's a hero. And that's why *I'm* here, to set the story straight. If you'll please just let me through.'

The pink-hatted lady mumbled something under her breath about ragamuffins running around London in their underwear, but she shuffled out of the way all the same.

'Thank you,' said Odelia pushing past on trembling legs. But now that she was actually here, with a scandal-hungry crowd pawing at the station door, her plan to come clean and confess everything seemed rather less attractive than before. It seemed downright terrifying, in fact. *What if they lock me up and throw away the key? What if I never see Mother or Sammy again?*

She pulled her lucky marble out of her shirt pocket and squeezed it tight.

'Please,' she begged. 'Please don't let them send me to jail.' But the marble, being a marble, said nothing.

CHAPTER 23

It was quiet and gloomy inside the station, the dark walls papered with scary-looking notices and pictures of wanted criminals.

'Hello again,' said a familiar-looking policeman at the front desk. It was Sergeant Thataway! 'Have you seen any more vultures? And how's that nasty cough of yours?'

I don't think I can do this, panicked Odelia. But then she pictured Captain Blunderfuss rattling his hook against the narrow bars of his cell, weeping for his old life at sea, and she knew she didn't have a choice.

'No-no,' she stammered. 'No more vultures. I've er … I've come to report … ummm …'

'The theft of your clothes?' guessed the sergeant. 'I'm assuming that's why you're dressed like that.'

'What? No, I've come about the pirate. Captain Blunderfuss, that is.' Odelia took a deep breath, clutching her lucky marble even tighter. 'It wasn't him who made the fake notes, that's what I've come to tell you. I mean yes, he might have cut up a few sheets of paper but that's not a crime, is it? At least, I don't think it is. The actual money-forging bit was all *my* idea. *I'm* the criminal mastermind of the operation. But it was only to get Sammy back,' she added quickly. 'A trick to catch the thieves.'

Yes, she thought. That sounded better. *Not a crime at all, just a trick.*

A loud clanking sound – like a prisoner in chains – came drifting in from the doorway behind the desk. A loud clanking sound followed by an even louder shriek.

Odelia shivered. *Toenails and terrapins! What's that? I suppose I'll find out soon enough if they lock me up too.* 'And it worked, didn't it?' she went on, quickly. 'I mean, you *did* catch the thieves, thanks to the captain. Which makes him a hero, not a villain. More of a champion than a varmint. So, if you could think about letting him go, that would be much appreciated.'

Sergeant Thataway looked Odelia up and down. 'Forging money, you say? A criminal mastermind? You?'

'Yes, exactly. Wait, I mean, no … I mean it *was* me but … but …'

'But what?' asked the sergeant.

'But …'

'Buttered toast and basking sharks,' finished a gruff voice. A gruff, gravelly, pirate kind of voice.

'Captain? Is that you?' Odelia looked up, hopefully, to see the important-looking policeman with the bushy eyebrows framed in the doorway. He was holding the biscuit tin.

Oh. Her hopes came crashing back down again.

For a moment there I thought it was ...

But then the important-looking policeman with the bushy eyebrows stepped aside to reveal a scruffy-looking pirate with an ugly big stain on his shirt. Not a bloodstain though, Odelia was relieved to see after all that shrieking. More like a tea stain. And there were no signs of any chains round his legs either ... In fact, the pirate looked decidedly cheerful for a man facing serious money-forging charges.

'Aye aye, Basin. It's me all right,' he said with a grin. 'I've just been helping the police with their cry-wees. And they've been helping me with a nice cup of tea and a biscuit. Sorry about all the clattering and squealing,' he added. 'I got my hook caught on the radiator.'

'You mean you've been helping them with their *enquiries*?' asked Odelia, relieved to see he wasn't wearing his handcuffs any more, either. Did that mean they were letting him go? Or did it mean the captain had told them what really happened? In which case *she'd* be the one in handcuffs soon ...

'Cry-wees. Yes, that's what I said. What are *you*

doing here, though?' asked the pirate. 'That's what I want to know.'

'I er … I came to turn myself in,' admitted Odelia. 'To set the record straight.' It was too late to pretend otherwise now. She'd already told Sergeant Thataway everything.

'Narwhals and nonsense,' said Captain Blunderfuss, with a brisk wave of his hook. 'There's no need for any of that.'

But Odelia had come too far to stop. 'It was all mine,' she confessed. 'The money, I mean. I'm the one you want. Please don't lock me up though. It was for a good cause, I swear. I only did it to save my brother.' *Oh Sammy!* Were babies allowed to visit prisoners in jail? The thought of him growing up without her was almost too much to bear.

'Really?' The important-looking policeman with the bushy eyebrows was all ears now. Ears and eyebrows. 'The money in the biscuit tin? You're saying it belongs to you?'

Odelia nodded. 'Yes,' she said, her voice little more

than a whisper. *This is it*, she thought. *This is the bit where they clap me in irons. Goodbye Sammy. Goodbye Mother. Goodbye sunshine and birdsong and the smell of roses after the rain* ... 'What happens now?' she asked. 'What are you going to do with me?'

'*Do* with you?' repeated the important-looking policeman with a smile, his eyes twinkling under his eyebrows. He couldn't have looked more pleased with himself if he'd tried.

You're enjoying this, aren't you, you crusty caterpillar-face? thought Odelia, bitterly. *My life is as good as over and all you can do is smile.*

'Well, I'll be giving you *this* back for a start,' he answered, handing her the biscuit tin. 'And then I'll be apologising for any inconvenience caused. I really am very sorry. You and your friend here are heroes – I should have seen that from the start. Fearlessly tackling the Mayfair Mob like that. We on the force owe you both a great debt of gratitude.'

'What? But the money ...?' Odelia stared down at the commemorative lid, trying to make sense of what she was hearing. 'I … I don't understand.'

'My mistake,' said the policeman. He was still smiling, but it seemed like more of an embarrassed-looking smile than a gloating one, now that Odelia came to think about it. 'For some reason I thought the notes were forged – it must have been a trick of the light or something – but on closer examination back here at the station I realised my error.'

'What?' asked Odelia again, feeling as confused as ever. She prised open the biscuit tin and peered inside to find it full of ten pound notes. But these were proper, crisp notes, issued by an actual bank. Not a single ink-smudge or wonky, home-drawn stamp in sight. 'I don't believe it,' she murmured quietly. 'Mother's writing must have worked its magic after all. It actually worked!' Relief flooded through her body. *That means I didn't forge anything – I'm innocent. I'm not going to jail after all! Oh, thank goodness for that!* And then, after the first flush of relief came a wave of excitement. Five hundred pounds was a serious amount of money, and with Sammy safe and sound it was all theirs. 'We'll be able to pay off *all* our debts with this.'

'With enough left over for a crate of marzipan fruits,' added Captain Blunderfuss. 'Actually, better make it two. My tum's emptier than a mermaid's trouser drawer.'

'But no raspberry ones,' said Odelia, grinning up at him.

'Bleurgh! Too right. If I so much as *smell* a raspberry in there – marzipan or no marzipan – I'll pickle his pips.'

'Don't worry, Captain, if there are any raspberry ones in there, I'll eat them for you. It'll make a nice change from toast.'

'It's a deal,' said the pirate, giving her his hook to shake. 'Come on then, Basin, let's get you home. The little feller will be wondering where you've got to.'

'You'll have to battle your way through the crowds first,' piped up Sergeant Thataway, peering through the window. 'It looks like half of London has come for a nosy.'

Captain Blunderfuss puffed out his chest. 'They

can nosy all they want. Let's go!'

The sudden rush of sound that hit them as they stepped outside was enough to make Odelia's ears ring. She'd never heard so many people shouting at once.

'There he is!'

'Look, it's the pirate! The one who held up the bank!'

'Watch out for his deadly hook!'

'It's the biscuit buccaneer – the one who broke into the biscuit factory.'

'Surely they're not letting him go free? The man's a killer!'

'Watch out, he's dangerous.'

'I'm not dangerous, I'm a hero,' objected Captain Blunderfuss. 'And anyone who says otherwise can walk the plank! I'll lily their livers and poop their decks!'

'No, Captain,' said Odelia, pulling him back. 'The police station *really* isn't the place for a fight. Let *me* talk to them.' She banged on the door with her biscuit tin, to get their attention, and cleared her throat. 'Ahoy there! My name's Odelia Harmony-Hardluck Smythe, and this is Captain Blunderfuss.

He might look and smell like a dangerous pirate but he's the *opposite* of a villain. He helped save my baby brother and single-handedly captured the leader of the Mayfair Mob in the process. And he saved me too,' she added. 'I was miserable before he came. We all were. And now ...' Odelia paused for a moment, considering the empty Father-shaped ache inside her chest. Yes, it was still there, but it felt smaller than before. Easier, somehow.

'And now out of our way,' finished the captain. 'I've got an important appointment with a crate of marzipan and a trunk of trousers.'

Father's trousers! 'Wait,' hissed Odelia, 'I haven't finished yet. You've given me an idea.' She waved to the reporters. There were more of them now, furiously jotting things down in their notebooks. 'Listen,' she shouted. 'You need to put this in your newspaper articles as well. It's very important that your readers get to hear this. I need you to write that the heroic Captain Blunderfuss tackled the villainous varmints while wearing a fine pair of Hose & Hope velvet knickerbockers. Because Hose & Hope knickerbockers are the trouser choice of heroes.'

'Should we compare him to *other* seafaring heroes?' asked one of the reporters. 'Such as Admiral Nelson?'

'Admiral Smellson? Don't even *think* about it,' roared the pirate. 'Or I'll have your fish guts for garters.'

CHAPTER 24

Two crates of marzipan fruits. (No raspberries.)

One crate of potatoes.

A side of salmon.

A goose.

A ham.

Carrots.

Onion soup.

Cheese turnovers.

Apple tartlets.

Almond tartlets.

Orange custard pudding.

Five different jellies – each one wobblier than the last.

A pineapple.

Fresh bread rolls.

Butter.

Biscuits.

Rum.

Five hundred pounds, it turned out, was enough to pay off all the family debts, redeem their pawned furniture, replace Mrs Ponsonby-Smarm's drainpipe and hedge, make a sizeable donation to the London Homeless Benevolent Fund *and* order in the most delicious, mouth-watering, stomach-filling feast Odelia had ever seen or tasted. Cook was in his element, baking, roasting, frying (and burning), and Dog was in his element, too, wolfing up all the dropped scraps from the dining room floor.

Sammy gurgled and chattered his way through the entire meal, exclaiming with delight at each new taste: 'Tarties! Jelly! Bic bics!' And Mrs Hardluck-Smythe seemed delighted too, now that the weight of all her worries had finally lifted. She was smiling and laughing like the old days. As for Captain Blunderfuss, well, he was the happiest Odelia had ever seen him, gorging himself on marzipan fruit and rum and singing hiccuppy sea shanties at the top of his voice.

'Yo ho, *hic*, and a bottle of rum,
Watch out marzipan, here I come.
The finest, *hic*, I ever did see,
Fit for a hero, *hic*, that's me.'

By the eighth verse, he was dancing around the table with a goose drumstick. And by the twelfth verse, they were *all* dancing around the table.

'Old Davy Jones had a jelly, had he,
Wobbling at the bottom of the deep blue sea.
With salmon and soup and pastries to spare,
And orange custard pudding in his pirate hair.'

'Again! Again!' cried Sammy, waving his chubby fists.

'All this dancing and rum is making me quite dizzy,' called Mrs Hardluck-Smythe as she spun around the dining table for the umpteenth time. But she wasn't showing any signs of slowing. 'Ankles away!'

'Ankles away!' echoed Odelia, feeling a warm glow of happiness from the top of her curtain headscarf to the tips of her buccaneer boots. Yes, she thought to herself, the number one best thing about having a rude, smelly, tuneless pirate for a friend *was everything*.

Odelia didn't see as much of Captain Blunderfuss in the days that followed – he was too busy helping Mrs Hardluck-Smythe with her book. But she could hear him all right, shouting out his suggestions, one after the other.

'Wriggling rabbitfish! Call that a fight? I'll show you what a *proper* fight looks like.'

'How about if the polar bear eats Admiral Arbuckle's trousers? That'll serve the pesky pilchard-pants right!'

'When do I get my cannon?'

She could hear her mother, too, laughing away as she wrote.

'Oh Captain, you are funny. Take that, you fart-faced flubberfish. Yes! That's perfect. Why didn't I think of that before?'

Odelia and Sammy were busy too, building a pirate ship in the front parlour, with curtains for sails and a metal ring from an old lampshade to steer them through the choppy seas.

'Watch out for that iceberg, Basin!' cried Captain Hardluck-Smythe. 'One-eared polar bear, ahoy!' And by 'iceberg', of course, she meant Cook, who was fast asleep on the ocean rug. And by 'polar bear', she meant Dog.

'Poly bear hoy! Spwat, spwat, spwat!'

It turned out that *playing* at pirates could be every bit as much fun as *being* a pirate, with a little buccaneering brother who was tottering around properly now. It was a lot easier too. No more run-ins with policemen to worry about. No more hedge holes. No more coaxing people down off the end of hooks. And when the pair of them were snuggled up in their homemade hammocks after a long day's sailing, Odelia would tell Sammy stories of her own, about shipwrecks and sealions and hidden treasure, sneaking in educational dictionary words beginning with 'u', like *unrivalled* and *unassailable* for the sheer fun of it. But she saved her best 'u' words for describing Captain Blunderfuss – words like *undisciplined, unappetising, uncivilised, uncouth, unethical, ungracious, unwashed, unkempt, unpalatable* and *unwholesome*. The pirate was all those things and more. But he was also *utterly, unreservedly unequalled* and *unforgettable. Unique.* And Odelia wouldn't have him any other way.

As far as Sammy was concerned, though, the pirate was still *Dada. Dada piwate.* His sister didn't have the heart to correct him. Sammy's real dada was long gone now, and all the pretending in the world couldn't bring him back. But at least Odelia knew how much

Mr Hardluck-Smythe had loved and treasured them – as if that was ever in doubt! Every time she reread his final diary entry it brought her a little less pain and a little more comfort. *Even in the midst of such misfortune, I'm still the luckiest man alive.* And perhaps, if Mr Hardluck-Smythe was looking down on them all now – as Odelia felt sure he must be – the fact that his family's short-trousered financial troubles were finally at an end was bringing him a little comfort too.

Thanks to the recent press coverage following Captain Blunderfuss's heroics, Hope & Hose velvet knickerbockers had seen an *unprecedented* rise in their share price. Any gentleman who was anyone could be seen sporting a pair, in black or mauve or peacock blue. A few daring ladies had been spotted wearing them too – looking decidedly handsome and dashing it had to be said – but Odelia still preferred her trusty old pirate bloomers.

Yes, the captain was quite the celebrity in Mayfair circles these days. Even Mrs Ponsonby-Smarm had been getting in on the act. 'Of course, I knew he was special the moment I clapped eyes on him,' Odelia heard her telling her posh friends over a garden tea party of cakes and cucumber sandwiches. 'Didn't I, Edward? "A pirate, in Hadlington Gardens? How marvellous," I said.' And Mr Pickfill the publisher had called twice in the last four days to see if Mrs Hardluck-Smythe had completed her manuscript of *The Adventures of Captain Blunderfuss* yet. He couldn't *wait* to publish it and had already offered her a contract for the sequel.

After so many months of empty sadness and toast, 17 Hadlington Gardens was finally a happy place again.

'If you'd stayed in your book where you belong, none of this would ever have happened,' Odelia told the captain, over a celebratory dinner of roast pork and apple sauce. Mrs Hardluck-Smythe had finally reached THE END on her manuscript. 'You made everything right again.'

'True,' agreed the pirate, modestly, picking a stray lump of crackling out of his teeth with his new silver toothpick. 'And it's been my best adventure yet.' His expression darkened. 'But I can't stay here forever, you know, Basin. I've got my own life to get back to. My boat. My rum barrels. My hold full of marzipan fruits and velvet trousers. Who's going to keep *The Sea Lion's Bellybutton* afloat if I'm not there?'

Go back? Even though deep down Odelia had known it was coming – fictional characters belonged in fiction, not real life – she still couldn't bear the thought of losing him. 'But … but …'

'Buttonhooks and bilberries,' said the pirate kindly, squeezing her arm. 'It's out of my hand, I'm afraid. Look,' he said, pulling the treasure map out of his pocket. 'The lines are getting fainter every day, and so am I. As for Cook and Dog,' he said, pointing to the sleeping pair on the other side of the table, 'they've barely got any ears at all any more.'

'It's the same with the money,' added Mrs Hardluck-Smythe, squeezing her daughter's other arm. 'I went to get the last of the bank notes out of the biscuit tin this morning, and they were looking decidedly fake. Whatever strange magic it was that brought our pirate friends here is fading.'

Odelia stared at the captain, hoping they were wrong. Hoping it was all a mistake. But the top of his tricorn hat was already a little fuzzier round the edges than before. And the black of his eyepatch was looking decidedly grey.

'I'll miss you,' she said, throwing her arms round the stiff stink of his food-encrusted coat and hugging him tight. 'Oh Captain, I'll miss you so much.'

'And I'll miss you too, Basin. But I'll be right there in the book if you need me.'

'And then there's the sequel, of course,' added Mrs Hardluck-Smythe. 'Writing is a strange, unpredictable kind of magic, Oddy. Who knows what will happen when we start on *The Further Adventures of Captain Blunderfuss?*'

'We?' echoed Odelia.

'Absolutely,' said Mrs Hardluck-Smythe. 'With the captain gone I'll need all the pirate help I can get.'

'Dada! Dada piwate bye-bye.'

'Yes, little feller,' said Captain Blunderfuss. 'I'm afraid so. Bye-bye for now, anyway.'

'We'll do you proud, Captain,' Odelia promised him, her mind already turning to fresh adventures. 'We'll make you the finest hero to *ever* sail the seventeen seas.'

'Aye aye,' he said with a smile. 'I know you will. You'll be a fine writer, just like your mother. But right now, you're still my basin. So pass me that last roast potato, you scurvy scoundrel, or you'll be swabbing the deck till sundown.'

Odelia heard him that night, just before she slipped away into sleep. Before the pirate slipped away to his old life on the sea.

'Sleep well, little Oddy Odd Sock,' he said, ruffling crackling-scented fingers through her unbrushed hair.

'Sleep well, Captain Blunderfuss,' she whispered back as the door closed behind him. 'Until next time.'

 THE END

JENNY MOORE

Jenny Moore is a freelance writer from Devon, writing for all ages from toddlers to adults. She was the first ever UK winner of the Commonwealth Short Story Competition and was shortlisted for the Greenhouse Funny Prize. Her numerous children's books include *Audrey Orr and the Robot Rage* which was selected by the Reading Agency for the 2020 Summer Reading Challenge. Jenny read English at Cambridge University and holds an MRes from the University of Strathclyde.

ELISA PAGANELLI

Elisa Paganelli was born in Modena, Italy, and since childhood has considered books to be her best friend. After a career in advertising and as an entrepreneur, she now lives and works in the UK as a freelance illustrator and creative designer, accompanied by her beloved pets. Elisa's award-winning books include *The Highland Falcon Thief* (Children's Fiction Book of the Year at the 2021 British Book Awards), *The House with Chicken Legs* and *Moon's First Friends*. Her aim is to work on projects linked to mental wellbeing, nature and animal rights. She feels most at home when she's out in the natural world and on her bedside table is always a pile of psychology books, and very often one of her cats.